witchnapped

an utterly suspenseful mystery novella

The Murderwell Mysteries
Book Six

b. g. wood

also by b. g. wood

witchnapped

chapter 1

. . .

The Taylor Swift of Paranormal Romance

Sometimes the biggest mysteries in life are the ones we hide from ourselves.

— Morgan L.F. Mallory

GINA BILETTI'S footsteps echoed through Haverford Hall's subterranean admin block as she made her escape.

After a summer packed with events—especially the monster that was the Summer Fête combined with Frau Loneskum's birthday extravaganza—she desperately needed a break. Even if that break involved letting Berenstein drag her to Portland for some witch-themed book signing.

The elevator hummed as it carried her up to ground level. She caught her reflection in the polished steel doors—honey-blonde hair now betraying more than an inch of dark roots that screamed for attention. She'd planned to squeeze in a salon visit during this Portland trip, but that would have to wait for next month's LA getaway with Danielle. At least the dark circles under her eyes were partially hidden by the fancy concealer gifted to her by Sam, Eliza's make-up artist.

The past few months had been a crash course in juggling

her duties as Hospitality Director—a job title that still felt like playing dress-up some days—with her unofficial role as the village's resident mystery-solver. But now, finally, she could take a little break.

The doors opened onto the South Courtyard, where the early September sun turned the Hall's sandstone walls to warm gold. The scene would have been perfectly pastoral if not for her two employees lounging by the back gate, creating their own private vape cloud.

Jared and Fallon stood in the late afternoon light, each with their own sleek device, chatting like old friends sharing a cigarette break in a black-and-white movie. Except with more tech and fewer carcinogens.

Note to self: no matter how tempting, never ever ever vape.

After what happened two weeks ago, Gina couldn't believe Fal and Jared were still at it. But she wasn't their mother, thank god, because she had enough trouble managing her own life without adding theirs to the mix.

"Heading out?" Fallon asked, her perpetual perkiness undimmed by fourteen-hour days.

"Trying to. Assuming nothing else needs crisis management before I reach my cottage."

"Not until the planning meeting next week," Jared said, adjusting his already-perfect tie with his free hand. He took a long drag from his vape pen, exhaling a cloud of something that smelled vaguely like vanilla. "Though I still can't believe you're voluntarily attending a paranormal romance reading. That's very off-brand for you."

"Trust me, I can't believe I'm going either." Gina shifted her bag. "But Berenstein hit me with those puppy dog eyes."

"The same look he gives customers who try to leave his shop without a new book?" Fallon's laugh carried across the courtyard.

"That's the one."

"Well, have fun in Portland," Jared said. "We'll keep things running until Tuesday."

Gina headed for the waiting electric vehicle, one of Maidenwell's ubiquitous self-driving cars. This one was part of the new batch that had arrived this summer—a cheerful retro-styled thing in powder blue and white, with a boxy frame and open sides that made it look like someone had shrunk down a vintage Jeep to three-quarters size and had given it a high-tech makeover.

"South end of the Village Green," she told the car's AI. "By the Tangles."

The village sprawled below them as the car wound its way down the hill, a patchwork of slate roofs and cobblestone streets that could have been plucked straight from the Cotswolds. After weeks of watching Maidenwell's population swell with Fête attendees, seeing it peaceful again made Gina smile, as if the village had exhaled and settled back into its true self.

The electric vehicle glided to a stop near the entrance to the Tangles. Gina grabbed her bag and headed into the maze-like shopping district. Weathered shop signs creaked gently overhead while the sound of footsteps and distant conversation echoed off the old stone walls. Every time she walked through here, Gina half-expected to stumble across a wizard's shop or a store selling dragon eggs. Though knowing Maidenwell, that probably existed somewhere.

She emerged onto St. Anselm's and made a beeline for the Chocolate Emporium. The familiar bell chimed as she pushed through the door, and the rich aroma of chocolate enveloped her. Her mouth started watering before she'd taken three steps.

Instead of Viv behind the marble counter, it was Elliott who stood arranging truffles in the display case. His dark mustache twitched slightly as he concentrated, reminding Gina of an artist contemplating his canvas. Which made sense, given that he usually worked in oils rather than chocolate.

"Hey stranger," Gina said. "Where's the boss lady?"

"Hospital." Elliott straightened up, catching her alarmed expression. "Nothing serious—just getting a weird callus checked out. Too much standing around making chocolate, probably."

"Jesus, Elliott." Gina pressed a hand to her chest, willing her pulse to slow. "Lead with 'nothing serious' next time, would you?"

"My bad."

"Tell her I stopped by? Though I won't see her tomorrow —heading to Portland in the morning."

"Ah yes, the great literary event with Berenstein." Elliot's eyes crinkled with amusement. "Millicent mentioned something about that. I bet you're wanting to score some road trip snacks."

"Uh, obviously!" Gina leaned over the case, where row after row of dark chocolate truffles sat like edible art, their surfaces catching the light with a sheen that made her mouth water. "What's that one?"

"New creation," Elliott said. "Juniper berry ganache in dark chocolate. Viv's been experimenting with local ingredients."

"Interesting. And potentially weird." She moved down the case. "Tell me about the honey truffles—are those new too?"

"Same recipe as always. Though we did switch to local honey from Rueben's place."

"Tempting, but I should probably stick with what I know works." She stood up. "Let me get a box of the raspberry heart truffles. And some of those chocolate-covered espresso beans. I'm going to need the caffeine for this weekend."

Elliott began carefully placing truffles in a burgundy box. "So who's the author you're going to see? Anyone famous?"

"Oh, yeah. Super famous. Morgan Mallory. She's basically the Taylor Swift of paranormal romance. TikTok worships her." Gina watched him tie a perfect bow with the gold ribbon.

"Never heard of her, actually."

"Not surprising—since you're not a teenage girl."

Elliott's mustache lifted in a slight smile as he added the bag of espresso beans to her order. "I am surprised Berenstein's such a big fan."

"Oh god, don't get me started." Gina rolled her eyes. "He's got an entire shrine to her books in his shop. It's a little sad."

"I take it you're not a convert?" Elliott asked.

"Berenstein gave me her first book for Christmas. I made it a quarter of the way through before the talking cat started quoting Shakespeare. That was my limit."

"Good to know. Well, enjoy."

"Thanks." Gina carefully nestled her chocolate stash into her bag—treating them with the reverence they deserved—and waved goodbye to Elliott.

Outside, the September sun had transformed the Village Green into a postcard-perfect scene. Couples sprawled on blankets while others walked their dogs across the grass, soaking up the last warmth of the day. Even Lisette Chen was out with her giant Bernese mix, both of them looking equally regal. The only thing marring the view was the small construction crew at the north end, clearing away the last remnants of the concert stage and pavilion from two weeks ago. Soon enough the Green would return to its natural state —just grass and trees and those beautiful flower beds the groundskeepers maintained with near-religious devotion. Gina couldn't wait to see it restored to the peaceful spot where she often came to think, especially on warm afternoons like this.

Her cottage waited across the Green, its honey-colored

stone glowing in the golden-hour light. Inside, she kicked off her shoes and poured herself a generous glass of Pinot. The wine was barely breathing when her keycard chimed with yet another message from Berenstein. That made what—seven today? Eight? She'd lost count somewhere between his anxious queries about Portland's weather forecast and his encyclopedic recommendations for restaurants they absolutely had to try.

She settled onto her couch and smiled into her wine glass. Berenstein might be the most high-maintenance friend she'd ever had, but his enthusiasm was infectious. And watching him geek out over his favorite author would possibly make this whole witch-themed weekend worthwhile.

Possibly.

chapter 2

. . .

The Art of Surviving Natto

THE NEXT MORNING dawned crisp and clear, another summer day that made Maidenwell look like it had been cut from a fairy tale. Gina pulled up to Berenstein's cottage in one of the larger electric vehicles she'd summoned fifteen minutes earlier. The sight that greeted her made her wonder if she should have ordered a moving truck instead.

"Who are you, Lady Gaga?" She stared at the parade of luggage Berenstein was wrestling onto his front path. "We're going to Portland for four days, not embarking on a world tour."

Berenstein adjusted his thick glasses, utterly unfazed by her judgment. "Portland is a very stylish city, my dear. And everyone at the reading will be dressed to the nines." He patted one of his matching leather bags with obvious pride. "Some of us like to be prepared."

"Some of us are insane," Gina muttered, but she helped him lug his small army of suitcases into the vehicle's storage compartment. It was only half a mile to the Maidenwell train station, but there was no way they could have walked with his mobile wardrobe—even on such a perfect morning.

The electric vehicle hummed quietly through the village's

narrow streets, passing locals heading to work and older residents taking their morning constitutionals. Gina stifled a yawn, her body protesting. She'd known better than to start that new true crime podcast series, but one episode had turned into four, and now she was paying the price. At least she'd learned some creative ways to dispose of bodies—though hopefully that wouldn't come in handy this weekend.

"Listen," she said as they approached the station, "I didn't sleep great last night. Mind if I catch some shut-eye on the train before our drive?"

"Pshaw! I've got plenty to keep me occupied." Berenstein pulled out his keycard, fingers hovering eagerly over the screen. "Need to catch up on my socials. The Trainverse is buzzing about Morgan's reading."

The 10 a.m. train puffed into the station like something straight out of *Harry Potter*, clouds of purely decorative steam billowing dramatically around its burgundy and brass facade. Gina had to admire the commitment to aesthetics—all that old-world charm hiding one of the most advanced electric engines in the world. The whole thing was peak Maidenwell: traditional on the outside, cutting-edge underneath. Inside, Gina claimed a window seat and let the gentle rocking motion lull her into what she hoped would be a restorative nap. But an hour later, as they pulled into Aune Station, she felt just as tired as when they'd left, and somehow even more aware of her own exhaustion.

The security screening went smoothly—they'd both done this dance before. Their Maidenwell keycards disappeared into a secure vault, to be held until their return. Then it was off to see Agatha, the elderly British woman who managed the station's "transition office" with military efficiency and grandmotherly charm.

"Here we are, then," Agatha said, her accent as crisp as her perfectly pressed blouse. She handed over their "outside" supplies: iPhones, wallets stuffed with credit cards and cash, and a key fob for their not-quite-rental car. "Do try to stay out of trouble this time, Miss Biletti."

"One slip-up," Gina protested. "And technically, that situation in Idaho wasn't my fault."

"Of course not, dear." Agatha's knowing smile said otherwise. "Have a lovely trip."

They found their car in the secure lot—a Kia Hybrid. *Big surprise.*

As Gina settled into the driver's seat, adjusting mirrors, reality sank in. Three hours to Portland. That meant three hours of Berenstein's running commentary on Morgan Mallory's literary genius.

She really should have gotten more sleep.

Just as Gina feared, Berenstein launched into a passionate dissertation on *The Witch on the Train* the moment they merged onto I-84. She tried focusing on the stunning Columbia River Gorge scenery instead—the towering cliffs, the glinting water, the occasional glimpse of windsurfers looking like colorful insects against the waves. But Berenstein's enthusiasm proved harder to ignore than the view.

"It's actually quite brilliant when you think about it," he said. "The way Mallory uses magic as a metaphor for self-actualization. Take Dahlia's journey, for instance—"

"I wouldn't know," Gina cut in. "I only made it through three chapters before giving up. Remember?"

Berenstein clutched his chest like she'd stabbed him. "Three chapters? That's practically literary abuse!"

"The witch was mixing love potions and pining over some bartender. Not exactly *War and Peace.*"

"Tavern owner," Berenstein corrected. "And it's so much deeper than that. The whole book is an exploration of identity and belonging. The way Dahlia questions whether she's running from the city or herself—"

"Speaking of running from the city," Gina interrupted, seizing her chance to change the subject, "how long have you been in Maidenwell now?"

"Coming up on four years." His expression softened. "Since the beginning."

"Ever miss New York?"

"Good lord, no." He shuddered dramatically. "The crowds, the humidity, the attitude. Though I do occasionally miss a proper nosh."

"Yeah, Libney's isn't quite H&H."

"But Maidenwell has other charms." Berenstein's eyes lit up. "Much like Danfeld Hills, where Dahlia realizes—"

"Nope," Gina said firmly. "We are not circling back to witch talk. Tell me about the bookstore instead. How'd you end up running it?"

But Berenstein was already diving into another passionate analysis of magical metaphors and self-discovery. Gina sighed and turned up the radio, letting his literary enthusiasm fade into pleasant background noise as the gorge's ancient cliffs rolled past. It was going to be a long drive.

Portland's Pearl District loomed ahead, all exposed brick and converted warehouses that screamed "industrial chic." The map app guided them to their destination, a chi-chi restaurant tucked into the ground floor of what had probably been a textile mill back when Oregon was still a territory. Now its weathered facade sported designer planters overflowing with carefully curated reeds.

"Just in time," Berenstein said, checking his watch. "Our reservation's in five minutes."

Inside, Bonu radiated the kind of understated elegance

that justified its year-long waiting list. The space balanced tradition and innovation as skillfully as its fusion menu—handcrafted teak tables gleamed beneath delicate paper lanterns, while abstract batik artworks in deep indigos and golds adorned the walls. The effect reminded Gina of those exclusive Manhattan spots where even getting the maître d' to acknowledge your existence required either a black Amex or friends in high places. Their server, immaculate in a charcoal suit, guided them to a corner table over-looking a miniature rock garden complete with trickling fountain.

"The seven-course natto tasting menu for both?" he asked, already reaching for his tablet.

"Just him." Gina pointed at Berenstein. "I'll stick with the regular lunch menu."

Berenstein's face fell. "But Gina, you promised to be adventurous!"

"Fine." She sighed, knowing resistance was futile. "I'll try one bite. One."

When the first course arrived—a delicate ceramic bowl containing what looked like beans drowning in cobwebs—Gina seriously reconsidered her life choices. The smell hit her first, a pungent wave that made her eyes water.

"It's all in the technique," Berenstein demonstrated, using his chopsticks to lift a glistening bundle. The strings of—whatever it was—stretched like rubber bands. "You have to embrace the texture of the natto."

Gina watched him pop a cluster of sticky fermented natto into his mouth with disturbing enthusiasm. Then, steeling herself, she snagged exactly one bean with her chopstick and popped it into her mouth.

It was worse than she'd imagined. So much worse.

"More sake," she gasped, grabbing the carafe. "Now."

"But the mouthfeel—" Berenstein started.

"Shut it!"

Forty-five minutes later, they emerged from lunch into Portland's late afternoon buzz. The Pearl District hummed with energy—cyclists weaving through traffic, packs of friends spilling out of brewpubs, tourists toting shopping bags and taking selfies. After months in Maidenwell's quaint quiet, the urban chaos felt oddly invigorating. Gina had forgotten how much she missed this—the pulse of a real city, the endless possibilities lurking around every corner.

"Coffee," she announced, scanning the street. At least there was no shortage of options—it seemed like there was a café every twenty feet in this neighborhood.

"What?"

"I need something to wash away the memory of those demon beans."

"But the reading starts in ten minutes!" Berenstein's hands fluttered anxiously.

"Relax." Gina steered them toward the nearest café, breathing in the rich scent of freshly ground coffee. "Powell's is literally across the street. Besides, if I have to sit through an hour of witchy romance, I'm doing it as hopped up as possible."

chapter 3

· · ·

World War Witch

CLUTCHING her Starbucks triple soy latté like a shield, Gina followed Berenstein toward Powell's. The late-summer air simmered with something more than heat—the unmistakable buzz of crowd tension. Before they could reach the bookstore's entrance, they found themselves caught in the crossfire of what looked like a small-scale culture war.

A knot of protesters had formed a human barrier before Powell's doors, brandishing signs with blood-red letters that screamed "PROTECT OUR CHILDREN" and "STOP SATANIC INFLUENCE." Their ringleader, a woman with helmet-perfect blonde hair and a face sculpted in righteous indignation, led them in a call-and-response chant about moral decay.

"Oh great," Gina muttered, clutching her latté closer. "Religious protesters."

"Family Values Majority." Berenstein's usual cheerful tone darkened. "That Karen leading them is none other than Robbie Jo Redding. She's made it her personal crusade to purge Morgan's books from every school library and bookshop in Oregon."

Gina made a face. The protesters—mostly middle-aged,

well-dressed, suburban types—had positioned themselves strategically to block the main entrance. Their signs were professionally printed, not handmade, suggesting organization and funding behind this "grassroots" demonstration.

Before she could share these observations with Berenstein, a wave of cheering erupted from the opposite direction. A group of women in flowing black dresses, crystal necklaces, and oversized pointed witch hats descended upon the scene, carrying their own handmade signs with pink triangles and various slogans: "MAGIC IS LOVE," "WITCHES FOR EQUALITY," "MY PRONOUNS ARE THEY/THEM/WITCH," and "KEEP YOUR ROSARIES OFF MY KINDLE."

"Let me guess." Gina arched an eyebrow. "The witch cavalry has arrived?"

"The Daughters of Aradia." He grinned, his earlier tension evaporating. "Morgan's biggest supporters. Bona fide Trainers. Look—that's Tara Diaz leading them."

A tall woman with striking purple hair and multiple piercings raised her hands, and the witchy counter-protesters began singing what sounded like an old folk song. The FVM group responded by raising their voices louder, creating a cacophony of competing chants that echoed off Powell's brick facade.

"Jesus." Gina took a fortifying sip of latté. "All this drama for a book signing?"

"Not just any book signing." Berenstein's eyes sparkled behind his thick glasses. "This is Morgan Mallory's first public appearance in over a year. And after that love potion scene in *Magicurious* went viral on TikTok—"

"Hey, is that Fred Armisen?" Gina said, trying to distract him. It didn't seem to work.

"Pshaw. This way." Berenstein tugged at Gina's sleeve, leading her around the corner. "There's another entrance on Couch Street."

The sounds of the chants faded as they circled the block. A young woman in a Powell's employee vest stood guard at the back entrance, checking tickets and ushering people inside.

"Thank god," Gina muttered as they showed their tickets. "I wasn't in the mood for a front-row seat to World War Witch."

The familiar scent of books and fresh coffee enveloped them as they entered. Powell's lived up to its "City of Books" nickname—the place was massive, with floor-to-ceiling shelves creating a literary labyrinth. Signs hung from the ceiling pointing to different colored rooms, but Gina might as well have been reading Sanskrit.

"The reading is up on the top floor," Berenstein said, practically bouncing with each step.

"Don't you want the elevator?" Gina asked. "I thought your knees were bothering you?"

"Steroid injections, my dear. Courtesy of Dr. Kurian. I didn't want anything to slow me down this weekend."

As they climbed to the Pearl Room, Gina thought back to last spring when Berenstein had pitched this Portland adventure. He'd been so excited about Morgan Mallory's reading that she couldn't say no, even though she wasn't a fan of these kinds of books—by any means.

"Almost there," Berenstein called from three steps ahead, his renewed mobility evident in his eager pace. The stairs opened onto a large room already thick with bodies and anticipation. "The Basil Hallward Gallery," he announced with reverence. "Named after—"

"The guy from *Dorian Gray*, yeah, I remember that much from high school."

The top floor's events space was already filling with bodies and the aggressive scent of patchouli. Berenstein secured them seats in the middle section while excited chatter buzzed around them. The women behind them conjectured about possible plotlines from Morgan's upcoming book with the intensity of sports commentators analyzing playoff strategies.

Towards the front, a group of the witchy women who had been facing off against the protesters were all sitting together (thankfully sans pointed hats), with the purple-haired leader right in the center of them.

"No wine at this thing?" Gina surveyed the room with mounting despair. "How do they expect us to survive a poetry reading stone-cold sober?"

"It's not—" Berenstein started, but his words cut off as the crowd suddenly hushed.

Morgan Mallory herself swept into the room, cradling a sleek black cat in her arms. The cat surveyed its audience with regal disdain. Morgan's vivid red bob caught the light, forming a fiery halo around her pale face. Her black ensemble hugged her curves, and silver jewelry clinked softly with each movement—rings on nearly every finger and a pentagram pendant at her throat. The small star tattoo near her left eye seemed to shimmer as she blinked, taking in the crowd with sharp green eyes rimmed in dramatic cat-eye makeup.

Okay…

At Morgan's shoulder moved a woman who immediately caught Gina's eye—not just because of her quiet poise, but because she was working that hip androgynous fashion thing that Gina knew she could never pull off. Her dark hair was cut in a sharp asymmetrical style, and she wore a stylish blazer over chic wide trousers.

"That's Ami, Morgan's assistant," Berenstein whispered, practically vibrating with gossip. "Though word is they're more than that. The Trainers are convinced they're secretly together."

"The who now?"

"Trainers. That's what the superfans call themselves. From *The Witch on the Train*. Get it?"

"Ugh. Kill me now."

"Hush, you heathen!"

But Gina had stopped listening. Her attention snagged on a ripple of tension near the stage.

Oh hello, drama!

Some guy pushed through the crowd—all prep school polish in his perfectly tailored sport coat (definitely Armani, if Gina's years of people-watching at Saks were worth anything). His face was flushed red as he made a beeline for Morgan.

"Morgan, we need to—"

But before Trust Fund Ken could finish, a woman materialized like some designer-clad ninja. Everything about her shouted "publicist"—from her Valentino glasses to her "I will end you" smile.

"Not now, Emerson," she hissed at the man, somehow making those three words sound like both a threat and a promise.

Their whispered argument carried across the room like the world's most awkward stage play. Gina caught fragments: *"…promised you wouldn't…"* and *"…can't keep hiding…"*

The guy yanked his arm free and stormed out, leaving a wake of raised phones and whispered speculation. There was definitely more to this story than just another entitled fanboy getting shut down.

Morgan settled into her chair as if nothing had happened, transferring the cat to her assistant with practiced grace.

When she began reading, her voice carried an unexpected warmth that filled the room like honey. The passage wasn't about spells or demons, but about lying awake at 3 a.m., haunted by choices between a sexy warlock and an even sexier ghost.

Gina had expected to spend the reading mentally reviewing last week's grocery list, but something in Morgan's words caught her off guard. She captured that middle-of-the-night emptiness perfectly—when your mind loops through every wrong turn, every missed connection, every what-if that led you here.

Gina stole a glance at the purple-haired woman—(Tara something?)—in the front row, noting how the witch activist's face flickered between rapture and something darker, more complicated.

After the reading concluded, the publicist announced that Morgan would be happy to sign copies of her books. In no time, a queue snaked through the stacks like a conga line.

Berenstein clutched his collection of books, practicing what he'd say to Morgan under his breath. After twenty minutes of shuffle-step-wait, Gina's feet ached in her new boots, and she'd counted exactly forty-seven ceiling tiles.

"Did you hear that part about the ghost's cold touch?" Berenstein whispered for approximately the eighteenth time. "The metaphor about frozen desire? Pure genius."

"Uh-huh."

As they inched closer, Gina found herself noticing odd details about Morgan that didn't quite fit her carefully curated image. Or maybe they did. Those nails, for instance—eight of them long and purple, but the middle two on each hand cut short and painted blood red. It was weird, but then again, what did she know about witch fashion? Her own boldest style choice was the tiny second piercing in her left ear, from Claire's at the Smith Haven Mall when she was sixteen.

At last Berenstein stepped up to the table, fumbling with his stack of books and delivering a breathless monologue about Morgan's influence on modern magical literature while she signed his small library of books. Her cat watched from its table-top throne, whiskers twitching with judgy energy. Then it was Gina's turn.

"Which book would you like signed?" Morgan reached for a fresh pen without making eye contact.

"Oh, I'm just the emotional support human." Gina gestured vaguely at Berenstein.

Then Morgan looked up, and the world tilted sideways.

Their eyes met, and electricity shot through Gina's body like a live wire. The room blurred at the edges, reality going soft around the corners. For one terrifying moment, a single thought crystallized with impossible clarity: *I'm not who I think I am.*

"Next," the publicist called sharply, but Gina couldn't move. Her legs had forgotten their basic function. The strange sensation pulsed through her in waves, leaving her dizzy and off-kilter. She might have stood there all night if Berenstein hadn't tugged her forward.

I'm not who I think I am. What was that supposed to mean? And where did it come from?

The rest of the signing passed in a fog. When the publicist declared they were wrapping up—but not to worry, Morgan would appear at tonight's gallery opening!—Gina barely registered the words.

Her mind kept circling back to that moment of connection, that impossible thought.

She'd experienced plenty of weird things in her life, but this was different. This felt like remembering something she'd never known she'd forgotten.

The publicist adjusted her designer frames with surgical precision. "Please remember to use our official hashtags— #WitchOnTour for today's reading and #TrainverseArt for tonight's gallery event. Your social engagement means every-thing to us."

Morgan rose from the signing table like a queen concluding court, the cat now curled in her arms. Her entourage moved with practiced efficiency—Ami the assistant gathering Morgan's belongings, while security cleared a path to a service elevator marked "Reserved." The doors closed on Morgan's enigmatic smile, leaving behind the lingering scent of her perfume and a room full of still-eager fans.

"Oh good, we're still on for the gallery, then," Berenstein said as they headed for the exit.

Gina stopped mid-stride. "What?"

"The gallery opening. I got us tickets last week." He pulled out a printout with two QR codes. "Surprise!"

"Yay, surprise," Gina muttered. The dull throb behind her eyes intensified. Of course, Berenstein would drag her to not one but two witch-themed events in a single day.

The Universe, it seemed, wasn't done with her yet.

chapter 4

· · ·

Plot Twist: It's a Pelican

THE DEMANO GALLERY was smack in the middle of Portland's Chinatown, but it could have been dropped right out of SoHo, with that restored brick and those cast-iron columns—total New York vibe.

Inside, though, the space felt welcoming rather than pretentious, with track lighting creating warm pools of light and temporary walls forming intimate alcoves filled with art and clusters of people.

As Gina stepped further into the gallery, she found herself drawn from piece to piece, each one more intriguing than the last. A woman in a vintage Pezband t-shirt stood before a video installation where ordinary objects—teacups, vases, a bird skull—rippled and shifted hypnotically on screen. She talked about her analog animation techniques to an attentive group, her enthusiasm infectious. In another corner, a Native artist spoke quietly about finding inspiration in Pacific Northwest forests as he gestured toward his painting of autumn leaves spiraling upward, transforming into moths or stars as they ascended.

The centerpiece was a massive dimensional painting where shadowy figures emerged from wisps of iridescent smoke, their forms caught between human and something otherworldly. The overall effect was both unsettling and mesmerizing, like walking into someone else's dream.

"Well, this is…something," she murmured to Berenstein.

He grinned, clearly delighted by her discomfort. "Keep your eyes peeled for the glitter cake."

"The what now?"

"Somewhere around here there's supposed to be a recreation of the cake from *Magicurious*. Rumor has it that it actually explodes. Rainbow sparkles and everything."

"Can't wait." Gina rolled her eyes. "I need wine for this. A lot of wine."

"Get me one too," Berenstein called after her. "I'm going to mingle."

Gina made her way to the bar, where a tall drink of water with a carefully curated beard was arranging wine glasses. His name tag read "Cody."

"What's good?" Gina asked.

"The Pinot's local. Furioso." He smiled just a touch too long while pouring.

"From *Mad Max*?" Gina asked.

The guy laughed. "Right? You're not the first to make that connection. But no, Furioso is a vineyard in Dundee."

"Is that around here?"

"Yeah. Less than an hour south of here."

"I'll have to put it on my list."

"You should. It's got a great vibe. And beautiful views." He reached for the wine bottle. "Can I interest you in a glass?"

"Better make it two, Cody."

"Both for you?" His eyebrows rose playfully. "I respect the commitment."

"As tempting as that sounds, one's for my friend."

"Ah. Boyfriend? Girlfriend? Friend-friend?"

"My sixty-eight-year-old gay boyfriend, actually." Gina

grinned. "He's over there comparing crystal collections with the witches."

Cody glanced across the room toward Berenstein and chuckled as he poured the wine. "Well, hobbies, right? See you soon?"

"Sooner than you think." Gina picked up both glasses. "I'm a fast drinker."

A voice interrupted Gina's shameless flirtation. "Excellent choice, ma'am. The Furioso Pietro is magnificent."

The man who had walked up beside her wore an actual velvet blazer and try-hard glasses that screamed art snob. Or maybe just generic snob. Gina vaguely recognized him from the reading.

"The Willamette Valley's terroir rivals Burgundy's," he droned on. "The volcanic soil, the marine sediment…" He gestured with his own wine glass, nearly sloshing Pinot onto his sleeve.

Cody caught Gina's desperate glance and stepped in. "Frank DeMano, this is—" He paused, realizing he hadn't caught her name.

"Gina," she supplied. "Gina Biletti. I'd shake your hand, but I'd have to chug one of these wines first."

"Oh, you wouldn't want to do that." Frank DeMano straightened his glasses. "The Pietro needs to be savored. The subtle notes of black cherry, the hint of forest floor—"

"Speaking of which," Gina lifted the glasses slightly, "I should get this to my friend before it loses its…subtle notes."

"Of course, of course." Frank swirled his wine. "And please, if you have any questions about the artwork, don't hesitate to find me. Each piece tells such a fascinating story."

As Gina wove her way back through the crowd, the penny dropped. *Frank DeMano. The DeMano Gallery.* No wonder he'd been lecturing about wine terroir like he owned the place.

Berenstein wrinkled his nose at the glass she handed him.

"I was hoping for something white. Something fruity and summery."

"Sorry, my friend. I'm not going back there."

"Oh?"

"Frank, the gallery owner, is hovering by the bar. And he's a talker."

Berenstein harrumphed. "I don't mind. I enjoy speaking to fellow shopkeepers."

"Suit yourself." Gina took a sip of her wine. "But hands off the bartender. He's mine."

"Darling, you can have him." Berenstein peered over her shoulder. "Though it looks like Frank's found his next victim. Poor soul didn't even see him coming."

Near a massive canvas depicting a spell casting tournament—all whirling leaves and crackling energy rendered in oils—Gina spotted the group of protesting witches from the bookstore. They all wore variations of sleek, androgynous outfits that made Gina's knee-length skirt and silk top feel dowdy. The purple-haired leader—Tara—commanded attention in a geometric black jumpsuit and clunky silver jewelry, radiating the kind of confidence that came from knowing exactly who you were.

"If he shows up again..." Tara's voice carried an edge of worry.

The others leaned closer, their expressions concerned. Before Gina could catch more of the conversation, the sharp click of heels announced the arrival of Morgan's publicist.

"Morgan and Ami are just finishing dinner," she announced to the group. "They'll be here any minute."

"That's Lauren Pope-Harper," one guest whispered to another. "She handles everything."

"Everything except keeping Morgan on schedule," came the reply with a laugh.

Gina found herself drifting toward a quieter corner of the gallery, where a large abstract triptych caught her eye. Thick black brushstrokes slashed across each canvas, wild and chaotic, as if captured mid-explosion. Jagged lines collided with bursts of white and faint hints of blue, creating an intense energy that seemed to leap off the walls. She felt as though she'd caught a glimpse of some strange, magical eruption, frozen in time but still vibrating with life. Her heart beat a little faster, caught up in the movement and mystery. It was raw, powerful, almost alive—and she couldn't look away.

"That's one of Harrison's."

Gina surveyed the woman next to her. Mid-fifties maybe, with this amazing silver-streaked blonde hair and fashionable glasses that worked perfectly with her pretty face and big eyes. The tiny diamond stud in her nose added just enough edge. Everything about her screamed 'cool art person who wouldn't judge you for knowing nothing about art.'

Gina peered at the small plaque beside the painting:

__Harrison Wood, "Arcanity IV"__
__Acrylic on Canvas, 72" x 108" (overall)__

"Do you know the artist?" she asked.

"I should hope so." The woman smiled. "He's my husband. I'm Bethany Wood."

"Gina Biletti." She was about to say more when a tall man in dark jeans and a perfectly tailored jacket approached with two glasses of wine. Obviously the husband. He was about the same age as Bethany, with full salt and pepper hair, intense eyes, and a short beard.

"Sorry for the delay." The guy handed one of the wines to his wife. "That gallery owner can talk your ear off about soil composition."

"Been there, done that," Gina laughed.

"This is Harrison," Bethany said. "Harrison, meet Gina. She was just admiring your work."

"The painting is incredible," Gina said. "You totally nailed the vibe of Morgan's books." She paused. "Well, from what I remember. I read three chapters of the first one. Don't tell anyone."

Harrison glanced around conspiratorially. "That's actually more than I've read." He smiled at her.

"What?"

"Not really my thing."

"Harrison's more of a Jack Reacher fan," Bethany explained.

"Same," Gina said. "Though only the Lee Child ones. The books his brother is writing just aren't the same."

"I'll drink to that," Harrison said.

Gina turned back to the painting. "Hold up—isn't this whole show supposed to be Morgan-inspired art?"

"Technically yes." Harrison's grey eyes danced with amusement. "I just pulled a random word from the first book. *Arcanity*." He motioned at the painting. "Seriously, it could be anything. A magic spell. Or a pelican."

Gina sipped her wine, letting the rich Pinot roll across her tongue as she studied the canvas with fresh eyes. "Sneaky. But yeah, now I totally see the pelican."

The three of them chatted easily about all kinds of things. Bethany had a way of making conversation feel natural, like they'd known each other for years instead of minutes. Or maybe it was just the relief of talking to normal humans instead of sparkle-obsessed witch fans.

"So do you live here?" Bethany asked. "In Portland, I mean?"

The gallery had grown warmer as more people arrived, the hum of conversation mixing with the soft clink of wine glasses.

"Walla Walla, actually. Moved from New York last year." The lie slipped out smoothly—Gina had rehearsed it enough times. "I work remotely for a tech company. Market research."

"I just retired myself," Bethany said. "Twenty-five years with Bend-La Pine School District. Now I'm starting a new chapter—literally. I've just started on a novel."

"Oh, like Morgan's?"

"Not quite. A mystery, for sure, but more realistic. With a little bit of humor."

"Oh, I could tell you some stories," Gina started, then caught herself. Could she really? Most of her recent escapades came with an NDA and a side of classified.

"We should grab dinner next time you're in Bend," Harrison said, pulling out his phone. "We've got some great restaurants in town."

They exchanged numbers, the moment of connection feeling surprisingly genuine despite Gina's necessary deceptions. After promising to be in touch, she excused herself to find Berenstein. The Woods seemed like exactly the kind of friends she would have made in her old life—back when she could tell the truth about who she was.

chapter 5

. . .

Now You See Her...

A RIPPLE of excitement moved through the crowd as Morgan Mallory finally arrived with Ami and her black cat. The author's dramatic entrance—all flowing black clothes and jangling silver jewelry—drew her fans like moths to flame. Ami was rocking a structured grey suit with military touches—sharp shoulders, dramatic buttons, wide-leg crops showing off serious boots.

But someone else caught Gina's attention: a woman skulking off to the side, her dated headscarf and tinted glasses screaming disguise rather than bohemian chic. The black wig with a red streak beneath the scarf didn't match the woman's complexion at all. Or her eyebrows, for that matter.

That preppy guy from the reading had also materialized, his pressed khakis still wildly out of place. He hovered at the edges of Morgan's crowd, never quite joining but never looking away either.

The two glasses of Pinot had caught up with Gina's bladder. Much as she wanted to keep tabs on the maybe-spy by the exit and Trust Fund Ken hovering around Morgan's fan club, she needed to deal with more pressing matters. Literally pressing.

She wandered toward the back of the gallery in search of a restroom, and eventually found it tucked down a dim hallway, past stacks of packing materials and bubble wrap. The door was locked, so she pulled out her phone to check work emails while she waited. The Summer Fête and Frau's birthday extravaganza had barely wrapped up, but her email was already drowning in frantic messages about Thanksgiving—as if anyone actually cared what color the napkins would be three months from now.

The lock's click echoed in the quiet hallway. The door swung open and Gina froze. A tall woman in perfectly fitted jeans and a simple black top emerged, and for one dizzying moment, Gina forgot how to breathe.

Her mouth formed the first syllable—"Car"—before her brain caught up. The height was exactly right, the athletic build identical. A stunning sleeve of tattoos cascaded down one arm. But when their eyes met, reality crashed in. This woman's face was softer, younger, her thin lips nothing like Carah's full, expressive mouth.

The almost-but-not-quite similarity left Gina feeling off-kilter, like someone had pulled the ground out from beneath her feet. She pressed a hand against the wall, steadying herself as the stranger murmured an "excuse me" and disappeared down the hall, leaving Gina to wonder why glimpsing Carah's ghost could leave her feeling so completely thrown off.

Inside, the small bathroom reeked of cloying vanilla and lavender from one of those plug-in air fresheners trying too hard. Gina splashed cold water on her face, the shock of it a welcome distraction from the lingering tremor in her hands. It was unnerving how strongly her body had reacted to that fleeting resemblance—her heart still hammering against her ribs.

She stared at her reflection, her own eyes wide and slightly unfocused. Should she go back out there? Another glass of wine to steady her nerves? Or switch to water? Her reflection offered zero helpful input.

On her way out, a gleam of a lens caught her eye. She glanced up to find a security camera aimed directly at the bathroom door. Something about its placement seemed off—who positioned a camera to watch people going to the bathroom? Maybe it deterred art thieves from stuffing small paintings down their pants. Still, the whole setup left her feeling even more uneasy.

Then a brush against her ankles made her jump.

She looked down to see Morgan's black cat weaving between her legs, radiating that distinctly feline confidence that declared all territory her personal domain.

The sight tugged at fond memories—she'd grown up with cats, but when she moved in with Erik, he said pets were a hard no, claiming allergies. She'd always suspected he just hated competing for attention.

The cat slipped down a hallway marked "Private," and Gina followed. Back here, the gallery's polished facade gave way to utility—exposed pipes, concrete walls, stacks of cardboard boxes. The cat sprang onto a box where one flap hung open, sending the cardboard creaking under her weight. When Gina lifted her off, the movement knocked the flap fully open, revealing dozens of identical paperback books inside. *Shanghai Revenge* by Dean K. Forman, the cover announced in bold letters. All the boxes bore the same label in thick black marker: "OVERSTOCK RETURNS." *Strange.* Since when did art galleries deal in bulk book storage?

"There you are!"

Gina turned to find Ami hurrying toward her.

"Little Miss Trouble!" Ami scooped up the cat and then turned to Gina with a grateful smile. "Thanks for catching her. She's obviously making herself at home here."

"No problem. I got worried when I saw her wandering off alone. What's her name?"

"Gertrude. Named after Gertrude Stein."

"Ah, nice." Gina hesitated, then added, "Your outfit is amazing, by the way."

"Thanks. I got it here. Fiercenail—this boutique in town. I always stock up when we're in Portland." Ami adjusted Gertrude in her arms. "Better get back to Morgan before she notices we're both AWOL."

After the drama with the cat and the phantom Carah, Gina decided one more glass of wine couldn't hurt. She was on vacation, after all, and the Furioso had gone down easy.

Threading her way back through the growing crowd, she found Cody the bartender deep in conversation with a woman who looked barely old enough to drink. Their shared laughter carried over the gallery noise.

Well, that ship had sailed.

The other bartender, a heavyset woman with close-cropped grey hair, poured Gina's wine without any of Cody's earlier charm.

After a long sip, she decided she'd do another lap of the gallery. Time to find Berenstein and figure out their exit strategy. All this witchy art was starting to feel a little claustrophobic.

She'd barely taken two steps when she nearly collided with Trust Fund Ken, wine sloshing dangerously close to the rim of her glass.

"I'm so sorry—" they both started at once.

"These crowds…worse than the bookstore," he said.

"At least here we have alcohol."

He raised his glass. "Exactly." His words had the loose edges of someone who'd been drinking since lunch.

"Wild guess—you're not a regular at witch-themed gallery openings?"

"Is it obvious?" He smiled. "The outfit give me away?"

"Among other things. I'm Gina."

"Emerson. Emerson Dalton." He took another sip. "In

from Boston, though I'm sure you couldn't tell from the accent."

The way he kept glancing at Morgan across the room—holding court in a cordoned-off alcove, admirers hovering—triggered Gina's curiosity radar.

"What brings you here?" She asked. "Art lover or Morgan Mallory lover?"

His face clouded. "Both. Neither." He swirled the wine in his glass. "It's complicated."

"Isn't it always?"

"You have no idea." Emerson's gaze never left Morgan. "We're engaged, actually."

The wine caught in Gina's throat. "I'm sorry, what now?"

"Not publicly, obviously. Can't have Morgan's fanbase discovering she's marrying—" he gestured at himself with his drink "—some boring investment banker."

"But I thought she and Ami…"

"All for show. Part of the brand." His bitter tone carried years of resentment. "Lauren makes me keep my distance at events like this. Wouldn't want to tarnish Morgan's carefully crafted image."

Gina watched Morgan laughing with her fans, one hand resting intimately on Ami's shoulder. The whole scene felt different now, like a play where she'd suddenly glimpsed the mechanics behind the curtain.

"That must be kind of weird…and difficult," she said.

"It won't matter soon, anyway. After this book tour, Morgan Mallory disappears forever."

"She's quitting writing?"

"Just retiring the pen name." He drained his glass. "And good riddance."

Before Gina could probe further, Emerson turned and melted into the crowd. She stood there, wine forgotten in her hand, mind spinning. The evening had just taken a sharp turn from merely strange into genuinely intriguing territory.

SHE FOUND Berenstein studying a massive full moon mosaic built from crushed glass and crystals. "I need to tell you something. About Morgan."

"Ooh, spill." He stepped away from the artwork.

Gina lowered her voice under cover of the gallery noise. "I just met her…fiancé."

"Her fiancé?" Berenstein's eyes widened.

"Guy named Emerson Dalton. Investment banker from Boston. They're keeping it quiet because of her image."

"But she and Ami—"

"Smoke and mirrors, apparently."

Berenstein absorbed this, the crystals forgotten. "Well, people can certainly love who they choose. Though some Trainers might disagree." He inhaled deeply. "When this gets out—"

"Don't look at me," Gina said. "I'm keeping quiet about it. Not my story to tell."

"Wise choice." He sighed.

"Sorry to interrupt."

Ami appeared beside them in a whisper of grey fabric. "Morgan would like a word."

Berenstein's face lit up. "Of course! I knew my analysis of the self-discovery metaphors in *Magicurious* would—"

"Actually," Ami turned to Gina, "she'd like to speak to *you*."

Berenstein deflated faster than a popped balloon. Gina shot him an apologetic look and followed Ami. Her wine buzz had evaporated, leaving behind a flutter of nervous anticipation.

Morgan was still hanging out in her VIP alcove, resplendent in her flowing clothes, Gertrude nestled in her lap. Behind her, a low table was littered with remnants of the evening—empty plates scattered with crumbs from hors d'oeuvres, half-empty glasses with rims stained with varying shades of lipstick, and an elaborate arrangement of white lilies.

Lauren the PR lady worked the crowd like a literary bouncer, carefully orchestrating which fans could approach their idol and when.

Hovering nearby were the Daughters of Aradia in their chic black outfits, purple-haired Tara whispering something to her companions. All of it felt staged, like a Renaissance painting of a queen holding court. All that was missing was the throne.

As they approached, Morgan caught Gina's eye and beckoned her closer with a small gesture. The movement sent light dancing across her rings, and Gina hesitated.

This didn't make sense. Berenstein was the one who'd actually read the books—all she'd done was skim one and chase after a wayward cat. Maybe Morgan had noticed her talking to Emerson? But no, they'd been well hidden in the crowd.

She gulped more wine and stepped forward.

"You rang?" The words tumbled out.

Morgan smiled, warm and genuine. "Sorry for the formal summons."

"No worries. Power move. I respect it."

Morgan's laugh cut through the gallery noise. "If I went looking for you, half the room would trail me around like ducklings."

"Yeah, I can see that happening."

"I'm Morgan Mallory."

"I kind of guessed. The cool black outfit, the adoring masses…"

They shared another laugh, and Gina felt her nervousness begin to dissolve. "I'm Gina Biletti. Is this about catching your cat earlier?"

"Gertrude?"

"Did you bring more than one cat tonight?"

The lightness in Morgan's expression shifted into something more focused. "Actually, it's about what happened at the reading. The…" She made a vague gesture in the air, fingers tracing invisible sparks.

The memory hit Gina with perfect clarity: that strange electric jolt when their eyes had met, like someone had rewired her brain for a split second. She'd convinced herself she'd imagined it, blamed it on too much coffee or not enough sleep.

Morgan leaned in, voice dropping. "You felt it too, didn't you?"

Before Gina could respond, movement at the corner of her vision caught her attention. Tara was leaning over the table, her hand hovering above Morgan's wine glass. A glint of something small and glass-like disappeared into her palm. Had she just—? No, that couldn't be right.

Morgan seemed oblivious to anything beyond their conversation, her dark eyes intense. "I know it must have been frightening. The first time it happened to me, I spent days trying to make sense of it. When—"

As Morgan reached for her wine, Gina's body moved before her brain could catch up. She knocked the glass away, sending red wine cascading down Morgan's black dress before the glass shattered against the floor.

"Someone just spiked your drink!" The words burst from Gina's mouth.

Morgan leaped up, wine dripping from her clothes. "What?"

"It was that woman—with the purple hair. I saw her."

The music cut out abruptly. The crash had drawn every eye in the gallery, and the sudden silence felt thick enough to choke on.

"Security!" Morgan's voice rang through the space. "Get her out of here."

Tara backed away, hands raised. "No, wait—it wasn't like that! I was trying to help you. It was just a protection potion, I swear!"

Two security guards materialized from the crowd. As they escorted a protesting Tara toward the exit, Morgan turned to Ami. "Call for the car," she said quietly. "I need to get out of here."

The look she gave Gina was complicated—gratitude mixed with something darker, more urgent. "We'll finish this conversation another time."

Morgan rose and asked where the restroom was. The gallery owner, Frank DeMano, swooped in and escorted her away, mumbling obsequious apologies.

Lauren and Ami circulated through the group, their voices a practiced mix of reassurance and deflection. The gallery hummed with whispered speculation about Tara's intentions.

Gina rejoined Berenstein and they slunk away from the action, parking themselves near a display of abstract paintings. That unfinished conversation nagged at her. Whatever Morgan had wanted to tell her about their shared moment of…what? Magic? Connection? It had seemed urgent.

Frank the gallery owner rushed toward Ami and Lauren, his carefully styled hair now distinctly disheveled. "She's gone."

chapter 6

· · ·

You're the One

"WHAT DO YOU MEAN, GONE?" Ami's voice carried a sharp edge.

"The bathroom's empty. I've checked the whole gallery." Frank's hands fluttered nervously. "And the back door was open—it shouldn't have been."

The news rippled through the remaining guests. Within minutes, the gallery dissolved into chaos as people spread out, calling Morgan's name. Their voices bounced off the high ceilings, mixing with the clatter of heels and the scrape of furniture being moved aside.

Gina drifted toward the restroom area, scanning the space with fresh eyes. Something felt off about the arrangement of artwork near the bathroom.

Before she could investigate further, the gallery's front door burst open. Two uniformed officers entered—a tall, broad-shouldered man with grey at his temples and a younger African American woman whose presence commanded as much authority as her partner's physical stature. Their navy-blue uniforms were starched sharp, duty belts laden with gear, body cameras blinking steadily on their chests.

"Everyone needs to clear the premises," the male officer announced, his deep voice cutting through the murmurs. "Now."

As the crowd filtered onto the street, the cool night air carried the wail of approaching sirens. Gina watched Ami pull out her phone, fingers trembling as she dialed. The Daughters of Aradia huddled together nearby, their earlier hostility replaced by genuine concern.

Something wasn't adding up. Morgan's cryptic words about their shared experience, Tara's potion, the convenient timing of Morgan's disappearance—it all felt connected, but Gina couldn't see the pattern yet. And now, standing on the sidewalk while police cordoned off the gallery, she had a sinking feeling this was just the beginning.

THE TALL COP introduced himself as Officer Banwo and asked Gina to walk him through the evening's events. The streetlamps cast stark shadows across his notepad as she recounted what she'd witnessed. Yes, she'd seen Morgan head to the bathroom. No, she hadn't noticed anyone suspicious following her. No, she didn't know Morgan personally.

"I did notice something strange," Gina said, then hesitated. How could she explain about the painting without sounding like she'd been snooping? "Near the bathrooms, one of the paintings looked like it had been moved—"

"We'll document any disturbances inside." Banwo barely glanced up from his writing. "Let's focus on what you observed of Ms. Mallory directly."

He ran through a few more routine questions and took down her contact info before closing his notepad with an air of finality.

After he moved on to question another guest, Gina spotted Lauren and Ami gathering a group of fans by the gallery entrance. They were pointing at a map on someone's phone, rallying a search party.

"I understand you want to help," Officer Washington called over to the group, her voice firm but kind. "But this area really isn't safe after dark. We've got patrol cars circling the blocks nearby. Let us handle the search."

"I'll call for a car," Berenstein said to Gina, his usual cheerfulness dimmed. "There's nothing more we can do here except get in the way of the police."

Gina nodded, though something about the whole situation felt wrong. They'd barely made their way to the corner when rapid footsteps approached behind them.

"Gina, wait." Ami caught up, slightly out of breath. "I… need your help with this."

"Of course we'll help," Berenstein said. "You wouldn't believe the mysteries Gina's solved. Several of them, actually. The police could learn a thing or two from her methods."

"Don't listen to him," Gina said. "I'm strictly an amateur—"

But before she could finish, Ami was tugging her away from Berenstein.

"Listen to me." Ami's whispered words sent a chill down Gina's spine: "This is going to sound insane. But Morgan told me something before she disappeared. She said you'd be the one to find her."

"What?"

Before Ami could answer, Officer Washington's voice cut through the night. "Ms. Fenton? We're ready to take your statement."

Ami pressed something into Gina's palm—a thick cream-colored business card. "We're at the Nines downtown. Call me in the morning?" The desperation in her eyes made Gina's previous doubts feel petty. "Please."

"First thing," Gina said, pocketing the card.

Ami hurried off to join Officer Washington, her boots

clicking against the sidewalk. The sound echoed off the old brick buildings, a lonely percussion in the night air. Gina watched until they disappeared into the gallery's warm light, leaving her and Berenstein in the shadows of a street that suddenly felt much darker than before.

GINA WOKE BEFORE HER ALARM, the events of last night still churning in her mind. She checked her phone and found a text from Ami.

> Morgan never came back to the hotel. Please call ASAP.

Her stomach clenched. She dialed Ami's number, pressing the phone tight against her ear.

"She's really missing," Ami's voice cracked. "I've called everyone, checked everywhere. Nothing."

"What about the police? Did they find anything?"

"No, and honestly, I don't think they are looking very hard. Listen, Gina, I know we don't know each other, but I could really use some help."

"I'll be right there." Gina swung her legs out of bed, already mentally cataloging what she needed to do. "I'll meet you in the lobby."

After gathering her stuff, Gina knocked on Berenstein's door across the hall. He answered in a hotel robe, coffee already in hand.

"Morgan's still missing," she said. "I'm heading over to meet Ami at The Nines. I'll be back for lunch."

"Of course. And Gina?" He paused. "Be careful."

The cool morning air hit her face like a slap as she stepped outside. A storm was rolling in, sending paper Starbucks cups skittering across the sidewalk while wind whipped between

Portland's old brick buildings. For a moment, the urban landscape reminded her of Manhattan. The thought left a sour taste in her mouth.

The Nines was only a few blocks away, located in an old department store building across from the courthouse. Gina rode up to the lobby on the eighth floor and when the elevator doors opened, she stepped out into a soaring atrium space. Light filtered weakly through the glass ceiling as drizzle began to spot the panes, casting muted shadows across the wide-planked wooden floors.

She spotted Ami standing near the reception desk, clutching a coffee cup. Gone was yesterday's sharp androgynous style—today she wore faded jeans and an oversized sweatshirt, and some simple glasses. Her distinctive asymmetrical haircut was hidden under a baseball cap with FACTS embroidered across the front, and the glasses didn't do much to obscure the dark circles shadowing her eyes. But when she spotted Gina, her shoulders sagged with visible relief.

"Thank god you're here." Ami's voice was barely a whisper. Gina felt a strange flutter of uncertainty—here she was, diving into another mystery with someone she barely knew. But looking at Ami's exhausted face, she couldn't help but feel for her. Being alone in a strange city while someone you cared about was missing…Gina knew from experience. That was hell.

They settled onto a velvet sofa in a quiet corner of the lobby. The art deco patterns beneath them swirled like frozen waves.

"I've been up all night," Ami said. "Most of it at the police station, filing reports and talking to detectives."

"Any leads at all?"

"Nothing." Ami's voice went quiet. "The cops did some preliminary checking with hospitals, looked at some street cameras. But they think she either left on her own or went off with Emerson."

"Her fiancé?"

"So you know about him?"

"Kind of hard to miss him bursting into both events. I actually talked to him at the gallery."

"What did he say?"

"That they're engaged, and—"

"He's not supposed to be talking about that." Ami pressed her fingers to her temples. Outside, rain gently splattered against the lobby's atrium windows.

"What does he think happened?"

"Says Leigh probably just needed to clear her head for a bit."

"Leigh?"

"That's Morgan's real name. Leigh Fay Dolan. Morgan Mallory is her pen name."

"Okay, tell me everything about her," Gina said, sliding onto the sofa next to her. "And I mean everything. Start at the beginning."

Ami wrapped her hands around her coffee cup. "Well, first of all, she's my sister-in-law. Ex-sister-in-law, actually."

"Are you serious?"

"Yeah, she was married to my brother Noah. They both worked for a big insurance company in Hartford. Leigh was in marketing; Noah was in sales."

"And how long were they married?"

"They barely lasted a year." A ghost of a smile crossed Ami's face. "But Leigh and I had gotten close. After the divorce, we started hanging out, going out drinking, complaining about work. She became my best friend."

"So you've known her for a while?"

"Almost ten years."

"And the whole couple thing?"

"Started as a way to keep guys from hitting on us at bars."

Through the atrium's glass ceiling, grey clouds drifted across the Portland sky.

"When did she start writing?"

"She'd always written, for as long as I've known her—women's fiction, domestic suspense, mostly. But she couldn't get any agents interested." Ami traced the rim of her cup. "Then one agent mentioned that paranormal was hot, especially with LGBTQ+ themes."

"That was the beginning of the witchy stuff?"

"Kind of. She went to Salem to do some research." Ami shook her head. "Said it was all tourist traps and tacky t-shirts. Have you been?"

"As a kid. Don't remember much except my parents buying me rock candy shaped like crystals."

"Well, it was on her drive back to Hartford that everything changed. She had a very weird experience."

Gina leaned forward. She had never been able to resist anything even vaguely supernatural. "Go ahead."

"There was this small town off the highway. She stopped for coffee at a little hole-in-the-wall café," Ami said. "There was a woman there, just a regular artsy type putting up flyers. But Leigh said when they saw each other, it was like being hit by lightning."

The hair on Gina's arms bristled as she remembered that electric jolt from Morgan at the reading. She was still shaken by it.

"Leigh drove home in this weird daze," Ami continued. "But suddenly the whole story for *The Witch on the Train* just appeared in her head. Characters, plot, everything—all fully formed. She said it was like watching a movie in her head."

"That's incredible."

"After that day, she started getting strange hunches and flashes of insight she couldn't explain." Ami's fingers fidgeted with her empty cup. "She was convinced that this book was going to be big. And when she sent it to the agent who had told her to write paranormal mysteries, she got signed right away. They shopped the manuscript and Leigh got a three-book deal with a really good advance. She quit her job and officially became Morgan. After that, she leaned heavily into the witch aesthetic, changed her hair, got tattoos, and really started getting involved in witchy social media. You've heard about WitchTok, right?"

"Not really." Gina rubbed her eyes, still processing the eerie similarity between Morgan's experience and her own. Minus the instant idea for a book.

"Things just came together after that. The first book was huge. The second even bigger. Topped all the bestseller lists for months. And I probably shouldn't tell you this, but..." Ami's voice dropped to a whisper. "A major streaming service bought the rights last year. They've already green-lit the TV series. So the franchise is about to get even bigger."

The rain drummed harder against the tall windows while Gina processed this information. A TV deal, bestseller status, rabid fans—it explained the pressure Morgan was under. And maybe why she'd disappeared.

chapter 7

. . .

Tell Me Everything

GINA CLEARED her throat and decided to steer the conversation back towards Emerson.

The simplest explanation was usually the right one—and what could be simpler than Morgan running off with her secret fiancé? All that pressure of maintaining a public image, living a lie…maybe she'd finally had enough.

"Tell me more about Emerson," Gina said. "What's the real story with him and Morgan?"

Ami shrugged. "Not much to tell. She met him at Trey Fergusson's party in Marblehead a year ago. They dated, fell in love, and they're supposed to get married next summer."

The memory of Emerson's slurred confessions surfaced in Gina's mind. "He mentioned Morgan's planning to retire her pen name."

Ami gasped like someone had dumped ice water down her back. "What are you talking about?"

"Emerson said after this tour she was done with being Morgan."

"That can't be right. She's been talking about a new trilogy, expanding the universe. With the TV series coming…" She shook her head. "No way."

"Could the pressure be getting to her, though? All those fans thinking she's someone she's not?"

Ami squirmed against the velvet sofa's overstuffed cushions. "The fans can get intense, sure. But Morgan thrives on it." Ami's voice hardened with certainty. "The only real stress is managing the Emerson situation. I keep telling her we need a plan for breaking it to everyone. It's not going to go over well."

"Come on," Gina scoffed. "These days? People can love whoever they want without judgment." Even as she said it, memories of judgment and expectations flooded back—Erik's mother's pursed lips when Gina used the wrong fork, the sideways glances at family gatherings in Alabama, his relatives asking what her "daddy" did.

"You'd think so, wouldn't you?" Ami's laugh held no humor. "Morgan has crafted this whole identity. The books, the witchy aesthetic, the queer representation—it's all intertwined. The art and the artist are one and the same." A slight blush colored her cheeks. "If you'll excuse my pride in calling Morgan's books art."

Gina crossed and uncrossed her legs, her mind wandering to her own messy life. That situation was different, yet somehow the same—the weight of others' expectations, the fear of judgment. She'd spent so many sleepless nights trying to untangle what it all meant, what she wanted, what she was afraid of.

But Ami was right—people's perceptions could make a prison of their own expectations.

Gina rubbed her temples. The lack of caffeine was making her head fuzzy. "Okay, so maybe she just got overwhelmed and took off with Emerson?"

"No." Ami's response was sharp, definitive. "She would never do that to me. Besides, I've been calling Emerson all night. Finally got through to him this morning."

Gina straightened in her chair. "Wait—he didn't answer all night? What did he say when you reached him?"

"Said his phone died."

"And you believe that?"

Ami shrugged. The confidence she'd shown moments ago seemed to drain away. "I don't know what to believe anymore."

"Where's Emerson staying? I'd like to have a word with him myself." Gina pushed herself up from the chair, ignoring her protesting muscles. Five hours of sleep and no coffee wasn't ideal for playing detective, but her brain was already clicking through possibilities.

It turned out that Emerson was staying at the same hotel as Gina—The Heathman.

"Small world," Gina muttered, gathering her jacket. "But before we go anywhere near him, I need caffeine or my brain's going to implode."

They ducked through the rain to the Starbucks on the corner of a cute little square nearby, where Gina ordered a triple latte and egg bite. While waiting at the pickup counter, she turned to Ami. "What about Morgan's phone? Have you tried calling it?"

Ami reached into her purse and pulled out a sleek black iPhone. "I always hold it for her during events. Morgan doesn't even carry a purse." She traced the phone case with her fingernail. "And before you ask, I already checked everything. No suspicious calls, no weird texts, no strange emails."

"Photos?" Gina grabbed her order from the barista and took a long sip of the latte. The warmth and caffeine began to clear some of the fog from her brain.

"Nothing unusual there either." Ami slipped the phone

back into her purse. "I've gone through it all at least three times."

They stepped back out into the drizzle, the wet pavement reflecting the grey morning light. "What about Morgan's PR person?" Gina asked. "Maybe she knows something."

"Lauren flew back to LA early this morning." Ami quickened her pace, navigating around a fresh puddle. "But I work closely with her. I can connect you two if you want to ask her anything."

Gina nodded. A PR person jetting off right after her client disappeared—that was either very convenient or very suspicious. She mentally saved that detail for later, along with Emerson's dead phone. The coincidences were starting to pile up like the grey clouds overhead.

As they rode the elevator to the sixth floor of The Heathman, Ami dug through her purse.

"Crap."

"What's wrong?"

"I thought I had my phone with me too. I must have just grabbed Morgan's. I was going to give Emerson a heads up that we were coming."

"Doesn't matter," Gina said.

The corridor smelled of fresh vacuum tracks in the plush carpeting, with lingering notes of someone's room service breakfast.

Ami rapped sharply on door 614. After a long pause, Emerson opened the door. He'd traded his chinos and button-downed shirt for a faded Harvard t-shirt and grey sweats that did nothing to hide the kind of sculpted muscles that sold overpriced rowing machines. Gina caught herself noticing, filed that observation under "extremely unhelpful," and focused on his bloodshot eyes instead.

"Has Leigh called yet?" he asked Ami, barely glancing at Gina.

"No," Ami said. "Can we come in?"

The room told the story of a rough night—tangled sheets, scattered pillows, a TV muttering on low volume. Gina caught the sour hint of stale alcohol underneath the hotel's signature citrus scent.

"Remember me?" Gina asked. "Gina. We met briefly at the gallery. I'm helping Ami look into what happened."

Emerson squinted at her. "Right. The wine incident."

"Can you tell us what you did after leaving the gallery last night?" Gina asked.

He sat on the edge of the unmade bed. "Went to a bar. Had way too many Old Fashioneds. Got back here around midnight, watched TV until I passed out."

"Your phone's been off," Ami said.

"Died last night. Just got it charging now." He gestured to where his iPhone sat plugged into the wall. "I tried calling her this morning, but she's not picking up."

"That's because I have her phone." Ami brandished the iPhone.

"Did Morgan seem worried about anything lately?" Gina asked, leaning on the edge of the desk. "Any strange calls or messages?"

"Not that I know of. She was just looking forward to this tour being over." Emerson turned to Ami with a smug expression on his face. "You know why, don't you?"

Ami glanced away. "I do now. But I'm not sure I believe it."

"Oh, believe it."

The tension in the room felt thick enough to spread on toast. "If Morgan—Leigh—wanted to get away from everything, where would she go?" Gina asked.

"Home, maybe? Her parents?" Emerson's voice held a note of uncertainty. "I honestly don't know."

"Camden," Ami said softly. "She'd go to Camden."

"Camden?" Emerson straightened up, his hangover apparently forgotten.

"New Jersey?" Gina asked.

"It's in Maine, actually," Ami explained. "On the bay. Leigh has a cottage there. Her grandmother's desk is there. That's where she goes if she needs some alone time for writing."

"Well, you learn something new every day," Emerson said.

Gina wasn't so sure about this. Maine seemed like an awfully long way to run from Oregon, but then again, sometimes the further you could get from your problems, the better.

"Does the cottage have a land line?" she asked.

"No," Ami said. "If she's there, there's no way to reach her. That's intentional."

"I'll go," Emerson announced. "Text me the address."

"Seriously?" The word just slipped out of Gina's mouth. "Don't you want to stick around here and help us look for her?"

Emerson shook his head. "She's not here. I'm sure of it. She doesn't even like Portland."

Ami shot Gina a look that spoke volumes about Emerson's cluelessness.

"Anything else?" Emerson asked. "I need to shower and get going."

"No, but let's all stay in touch," Gina said.

The elevator descended in silence. Gina was lost in her own thoughts and apparently so was Ami. In the lobby a jazz rendition of some pop song played softly in the background.

"Listen," Gina said quietly. "If Morgan's not with Emerson, I think there's a good chance that she was taken against her will."

Ami's shoulders tensed. "I've been trying not to think about that possibility. But yes, you're right. There is no way she'd go off on her own without telling me."

"We need to contact Lauren and the publisher right away.

If this is a kidnapping, the person responsible will probably try to make contact soon."

"Oh god." Ami pressed her hand against her mouth.

"We have to move fast. The first twenty-four hours are crucial." Gina paused, letting that sink in. "And one thing we know for certain—if Morgan was taken, it happened at the gallery. I'm going to head over there."

"I'll come with you."

"No. We need to divide and conquer. Can you handle Lauren and the publisher? Also review the guest list. Look for any names that seem out of place."

"Sure."

"And can you send me the gallery owner's information? Frank something, right?"

"DeMano, yes. As soon as I'm reunited with my phone."

chapter 8

· · ·

That's No Rat

GINA TOOK the elevator back to the fourth floor where Berenstein was staying.

"Rise and shine, old man," she called, knocking on his door. "We've got a gallery to investigate."

Berenstein opened the door, already dressed in a fresh button-down shirt and cardigan. The room behind him smelled of chamomile tea and hotel soap. "Give me two minutes to finish my morning crossword."

"Seriously?"

"Four letters, 'author's output.' It's not 'book.' I'm stuck."

"*Work*. And we need to get moving."

Thankfully, the rain had petered out by the time they left the hotel, though puddles still dotted the sidewalk. The moisture in the air felt foreign after months in Maidenwell's high desert climate, where rain barely lasted long enough to dampen the ground.

Though the gallery was less than a mile away, Gina had called for an Uber, asking him to drop them off a block early so she could get a sense of the neighborhood.

"Is this considered Chinatown?" she asked as the car pulled over in front of a black-windowed "gentlemen's club."

The Uber driver nodded. "Yeah. Chinatown or Old Town. Either way, it's the oldest part of the city."

Through the morning mist, weathered brick buildings stretched toward grey skies. Gina noticed identical gold lettering on several buildings—historical markers documenting their past: *Erickson Saloon 1912. Couch Block 1906.*

A man wrapped in a blue tarp slept in a doorway, surrounded by overflowing shopping carts. A group huddled around a burning trash can in an alley, their voices carrying in the damp air.

Berenstein shifted uncomfortably. "If Morgan did wander off last night…this isn't the safest area to get lost in."

"Don't worry, I'll protect you," Gina said, steering them down the wet sidewalk. The DeMano Gallery loomed ahead, its windows dark and metal security gate firmly locked.

Berenstein approached the door and rattled it for good measure. "Locked up tighter than King Tut's tomb before Carter came knocking."

"Well, this is disappointing but not unexpected," Gina said. "The sign says 'By Appointment Only.'"

"Now can we please relocate somewhere less concerning?" Berenstein asked.

"Not so fast." Gina pointed to a small mini-market on the corner, its barred windows cluttered with faded cigarette ads and lottery signs. "Let's pop in here."

"You hankering for a Slim Jim or something?" Berenstein asked.

"Sometimes the best way to learn about a business is to ask its neighbors."

The bell above the door jangled as they entered the cramped space that smelled of incense and day-old coffee.

The small space held all the familiar sights and smells of the corner markets Gina remembered from New York's Chinatown—a riot of American candy bars and lottery tickets sharing cramped shelf space with mysterious Chinese snacks and gnarled root vegetables she couldn't name. A giant rack of cheap jewelry glittered in one corner, while a dusty aquarium bubbled away in another, its dim light barely penetrating the shadows between the packed shelves. The smell hit her with a wave of nostalgia: sweet incense mixing with dried fish and exotic spices, exactly like those little markets in Chinatown where she used to buy emergency midnight snacks and questionable produce.

But the guy behind the counter wasn't who she'd expected in a traditional Chinese market. Young, with dreadlocks and thick-rimmed hipster glasses, he scrolled through his phone with a bored air.

"Working hard or hardly working?" Gina sidled up to the counter with a smile.

"Huh?"

"Hi, I'm Gina and this is Larry. We were wondering if you'd heard about what happened at the gallery last night. The missing author?"

His eyes narrowed slightly. "Why're you asking?"

"We're part of a citizen's group helping to find her." It wasn't technically a lie. They were citizens. In a group. Trying to find Morgan. "Your name is…?"

"Tamar."

"Nice to meet you, Tamar. Were you working last night? At around eight?"

"We close at seven, and I spoke to the cops already." He adjusted his glasses. "Didn't see anything. Only people that came in were folks from the neighborhood."

Gina nodded. She hadn't expected Morgan to pop in here, but it was worth checking. She tried another tack. "You know Frank DeMano? The gallery owner?"

"Not really. He comes in for kombucha sometimes. That's about it."

"Any other gallery employees?" Gina asked.

"Pretty much just Frank these days. Don't think the place

is doing that great. Might be going out of business. Or at least giving up their lease. But don't quote me on that."

Gina tried to recall any other staff from the previous night. There had been bartenders, servers—but they could have been from the catering company. The gallery had seemed successful enough, with its fancy wine and well-dressed crowd.

"Out of business?" Berenstein leaned against the counter. "Place was packed last night."

"One good night doesn't pay the bills." Tamar wiped down the counter with a rag that had seen better days. "But if you really want to know what's up, talk to my aunt. She owns the building, knows Frank and his wife pretty well."

Wife? A mental image of Frank from last night flashed through Gina's mind—no ring, no mention of a spouse, definitely giving off single-man-about-town vibes.

"Would your aunt be willing to talk to us?"

"You actually just missed her." Tamar grabbed a business card from under the counter and scribbled on the back. "Here's her number."

"Thanks, this is really helpful."

"Seems like you're more interested in real estate than finding that lady." He drummed his fingers on the counter. "No judgment though."

"We're very much interested in finding Morgan," Gina said firmly. She glanced out at the street where two men were arguing over an empty can. "The cops warned us against sending out a search party last night. Is this really a bad area?"

"You must not be from around here."

"We're not."

"Well, during the day it's not too bad. But keep your eyes open, you know? Some folks around here are desperate. And desperate people do desperate things."

The bell over the door rang again, and they all turned. For

a split second, Gina's heart leapt—but instead of Morgan, a tall woman with close-cropped iron-grey hair swept in. She kind of looked like Shari Belafonte.

"Tamar, did I leave that stack of mail here?"

"Speak of the devil." Tamar grinned at Gina. "Aunt Dee, these people were just asking about Frank DeMano."

The woman's sharp gaze shifted to Gina and Berenstein. Up close, her face had the same angular features as her nephew, though decades of experience had carved deeper lines around her mouth.

"Hello, I'm Gina Biletti, and this is Larry."

"Dee Lokumbe. What's this all about?"

"We're trying to find out what happened to an author who disappeared from Frank's gallery last night."

Dee crossed her arms. "Yeah, I read about that on Nextdoor. But Frank won't be much help—he's in Miami."

"Miami?" The word dropped like a stone in Gina's stomach. With a missing person and a possible crime scene in his gallery, she'd expected Frank to stick around.

"That's what he told me when I tried to schedule a time this week to take some measurements. Said he had urgent business."

Something clicked in Gina's mind. "Frank told the police he found the back door open right after Morgan disappeared," she said.

"You think she just slipped out?" Dee asked.

"Or someone slipped in." The chill from the store's ancient air conditioner raised goosebumps on Gina's arms. "And took her."

Dee shifted her weight. "There's an easy way to check. Every alley door has a security camera mounted above it—insurance requirement."

Finally. After hours of dead ends and frustration, a real lead dangled in front of them. "Could you show us?"

"Come on." Dee gestured for them to follow.

She led them through a narrow corridor. It smelled like wet cardboard and ancient spices. The passage twisted past stacks of empty produce crates before ending at a heavy metal service door.

The alley behind the building felt like stepping back in time. The old brick walls rose three stories on either side, their surfaces dotted with rusted fire escapes and ancient painted advertisements barely visible through a century of grime. Someone had sprayed fresh graffiti across a dumpster—bright pink letters that seemed to vibrate against the surrounding grey.

Dee stopped at a door marked 121 and pointed upward. "There's your security camera."

The camera hung askew from its mount above the door, its lens pointing more at the brick wall than the space below. Rain had left dark streaks down the metal casing.

"Has it always been like that?" Gina asked. The whole setup looked about as secure as a screen door on a submarine.

"Not sure. To be honest, I don't check it very often." Dee shrugged. "When I get back to my office, I can find the footage for you. What time did you say she went missing?

"Around eight," Gina said. "I really appreciate your help. A lot of people are really freaked out that Morgan's gone missing."

They exchanged numbers, and Dee headed off to her next appointment with a quick wave and a "good luck with your search."

As they walked back toward the street, Gina spotted something dark and furry near the dumpster. "Great, because this situation isn't creepy enough without the mutant Portland rats."

"That's no rat." Berenstein stepped closer, squinting through his thick glasses.

Behind a wet cardboard box lay a black wig with a streak of red running through the bangs. It was the same distinctive streak Gina had noticed last night, bobbing through the crowded gallery like a warning flag.

Berenstein extended his umbrella like a fencing foil, using the tip to hook the wig from behind the cardboard box. He lifted it high, raindrops pattering against the synthetic fibers.

The sight of the wig dangling there sent an involuntary shiver down Gina's spine. Last night it had been perched atop someone's head. Now it looked defeated, bedraggled. She pulled out her phone. "Hold it still."

Her hands weren't quite steady as she snapped the photo. The image captured the red streak perfectly, a slash of crimson against the wet black strands. She started to text it to Ami.

"What should I do with this thing?" Berenstein asked, still holding the umbrella aloft.

"One second." Gina pressed Ami's contact and waited for the call to connect. It went right to voicemail.

"Ami? It's Gina. I'm sending you something. Can you check the social feeds from last night? Look for anyone wearing a black wig with a red streak. She had on a head-scarf, tinted glasses."

"Incoming!" Berenstein shouted, his voice full of mischief.

The wig sailed through the air toward her face. Gina's shriek echoed off the brick walls as she batted it away.

"Sorry," Berenstein said. "It slipped."

"You are so dead!"

chapter 9

. . .

STILL GRUMBLING about Berenstein's wig assault, Gina reluctantly agreed when he insisted they needed a lunch break. They caught an Uber across the river to the east side, where he'd been drooling over some restaurant's Instagram posts for months. Food, apparently, was his peace offering.

Kaeros was a trendy Middle Eastern restaurant with curved archways, giant globular fish tanks, brass fixtures, and millennial pink walls. The place buzzed with the kind of energy that was a world away from Maidenwell's quaint eateries. Gina had to admit, the grilled halloumi with pomegranate molasses lived up to the hype, and the cocktail menu demanded exploration.

"Okay, I'm impressed you found this place." She took a sip of her Saffron Mojito—rum and mint mingled with golden threads of spice. The warmth lingered pleasantly on her tongue.

"The food pics looked amazing." Berenstein dabbed hummus from his beard. "I really couldn't resist."

The restaurant's playlist shifted from indie rock to something vaguely Indian as Gina pushed her food around the plate. "Don't you think it's sketchy that Frank took off to

Miami right after Morgan disappeared? And that security camera—"

"I don't think Frank had anything to do with this."

"What?"

"You're looking at this all wrong, my dear." Berenstein set down his fork with the authority that came from decades of recommending mystery novels to picky readers.

"How so?"

"*Means, Motive, Opportunity.* The holy trinity of solving any crime." He gave her that same knowing look he'd given her two weeks ago when they'd puzzled over the Eliza thing. Back then, his methodical approach had helped Gina eliminate a suspect, but whatever.

"I know that." The mint leaves in her second Saffron Mojito swirled as she stirred the ice with her straw.

"Then you know Motive comes first. Without a compelling reason, Means and Opportunity are just circumstantial noise."

"And your point is?"

"What possible motive would Frank have for kidnapping Morgan? Her presence at the gallery had to be a huge draw. Potential buyers, press coverage, social media buzz—exactly what a struggling business needs. It just doesn't make sense."

"So if you don't think Frank's our man, who is?"

"Well, nothing says 'sketchy' quite like a hastily discarded wig in an alley."

"Have to agree with you there," Gina said. "But let's not forget the pissed-off witches."

"Ah yes, Tara Diaz and the Daughters of Aradia. They may or may not have tried to poison Morgan. If you're curious, the Daughters are having a meet-up tonight, actually." Berenstein swiped the last piece of flatbread through the remains of his labneh.

"And how exactly do you know that?"

"I follow them on TikTok, of course." He shrugged at

Gina's look of disbelief. "These girls are way more into the Trainverse than me. Makes me look like a mere dilettante, to be honest."

A server cleared their empty plates, the ceramic clattering against the brass railing of her cart. The sound mingled with the conversation and laughter that bounced off the pink walls, creating a sophisticated din that reminded Gina of Manhattan restaurants.

"If they're such hardcore fans, maybe they decided to take their devotion to the next level," she said. "Like kidnapping the object of their obsession."

"Not beyond the realm of possibility," Berenstein said. "They very well might believe they are protecting Morgan. Doing it for her own good."

Gina remembered Tara's expression when she caught her messing with Morgan's drink. "We should definitely crash their meet-up. Get a read on them."

"I'm afraid you're on your own for this one." Berenstein pulled out his phone and scrolled through something. "It's women-only."

"Are you serious?"

"Perfectly. The Daughters are all about 'Girl Power plus Witch Power.' They'd never let a Y chromosome get past the front door."

A group of 20-something women at the next table burst into laughter over something on their phones. The sound echoed off the archways above, momentarily drowning out the music.

"Great. So, where are you sending me all alone?"

"Clover & Crow. It's this witchy bookstore and apothecary." He showed her the TikTok post. "They do tarot readings and sell crystals alongside their books. Very on-brand for the Daughters."

"I could do some tarot," Gina said. The pieces were falling into place. Between the wig in the alley and whatever had gone down with that drink at the gallery, the Daughters of Aradia definitely had some explaining to do. And she intended to get answers, even if she had to wade through a sea of crystal-clutching wannabe witches to do it.

Berenstein gave her a concerned look. "Just be careful. These women take their craft very seriously…"

"Don't worry." Gina waved down the server for their check. "I won't accept any suspicious beverages from strangers, magical or otherwise."

BACK AT THE HOTEL, Berenstein mumbled something about needing a nap and shuffled off to his room. The saffron mojitos had left Gina pleasantly buzzed, but not enough to ignore the stack of unread texts on her phone.

The first was from Millicent:

> Any chance you'd be up for some pet sitting next month? Elliott just announced that the SF trip is back on!

The message brought a smile to Gina's face. A few weeks ago, Millicent had been convinced Elliott was planning to propose during their San Francisco getaway. He'd made a big show of getting tickets to see Zepparella, his favorite all-girl Led Zeppelin tribute band, but there had been all these little signs—most notably catching him suspiciously rifling through her jewelry box, probably trying to figure out her ring size.

Then on Monday, he'd abruptly cancelled, muttering something about an emergency at the Chocolate Emporium.

Millicent had acted surprisingly chill about the whole thing. After her disaster of an engagement several years ago —finding out her mother had practically scripted the whole relationship, right down to coaching her then-fiancé on how to propose—Millicent had developed a significant phobia about making things official with a guy.

But now the trip was back on. Gina's thumbs flew across her phone screen:

> Count me in. I want all the deets when I get back!

She loved Pixel, the tiny grey cat who'd become the unofficial mascot of Millicent's paper studio. Cat-sitting her would be a joy.

Gina kicked off her shoes and stretched out on the hotel bed, the crisp white duvet cool against her arms. The Portland rain had started up again, a gentle rhythm against the window that nearly lulled her into closing her eyes. Then her phone buzzed again.

But it wasn't Millicent. It was Ami:

> Found our mystery woman in the wig. You're going to want to see this.

The rain had diminished to a light mist by the time Gina arrived at Ami's hotel suite. The room was twice the size of her own, with floor-to-ceiling windows overlooking the courthouse square.

"Morgan likes to travel in style," Ami said, catching Gina's glance at the oversized room.

"Apparently."

Ami led her to a sitting area where a laptop was set up on a coffee table. As they sat down on the sofa, Morgan's cat Gertrude emerged from beneath the table, stretching languidly. The cat fixed Gina with the same intense stare from the gallery, then leaped onto the sofa beside her.

"Oh, hello." Gina reached out tentatively, and to her

surprise, Gertrude bumped her head against Gina's hand, demanding attention.

"She's usually a little iffy with strangers," Ami said, watching with raised eyebrows as Gertrude settled into Gina's lap. "Seems to like you, though."

The warmth of the cat's purring body felt oddly comforting amid the uncertainty surrounding Morgan's disappearance.

Ami turned the laptop. "Look at this."

The screen showed an Instagram grid filled with photos from the gallery opening. Ami clicked through several posts tagged with #WitchOnTour and #TrainverseArt until she found what she was looking for—a shot of the mysterious woman in oversized sunglasses and a dark wig with the red streak, mingling with other guests. Her tailored black suit and white dress shirt stood out among the hipper attire of the crowd.

"That's definitely her," Gina said. "I remember that headscarf."

Ami's fingers moved across the trackpad, pulling up another set of images. These showed the protest outside Powell's, where the Family Values Majority had gathered with their signs. At the center of the group stood a woman in an identical black suit—but instead of a dark wig, she had the kind of immaculate blonde bob that suggested weekly salon visits and industrial-strength hairspray.

"Hold up." Gina leaned closer to the screen, her stomach doing a weird flip. "That's the same woman?" The name floated just out of reach, even though Berenstein had filled her in during their front-row seat to the protest drama. "Who is she again?"

"Robbie Jo Redding." Ami's voice had an edge to it. "She runs the Portland chapter of Family Values Majority. We got a heads-up about her."

Gina studied Robbie Jo's stern expression in the protest

photo. There was something unsettling about someone who could pivot from leading an anti-witch demonstration to lurking around Morgan's art opening in disguise. That kind of zealotry could easily turn dangerous.

"What if she wasn't just there to spy?" Gina said. "What if she wanted to do more than protest?"

"I know. That's what I'm afraid of." Ami's shoulders tensed as she stared at the screen. "We need to find her."

"Where do we start?"

"Already on it." Ami pulled up a new browser tab. The LinkedIn page showed Robbie Jo's corporate headshot, complete with a pearls-and-sweater set ensemble that screamed middle management. "When she's not burning books, she manages a Crafty Cloister in Beaverton."

Of course she does. The craft store chain was notorious for its conservative Christian stance, making headlines with their Supreme Court battles over women's health and fair treatment of LGBTQ+ employees and customers. Gina shuddered at the thought of walking into one of their stores, but finding Morgan was more important than her principles.

"I've got a rental car," Gina said. "Can you navigate?"

"Absolutely." Ami grabbed her bag. "Let's go talk to the crusader."

chapter 10

. . .

Have a Blessed Day

THE LATE AFTERNOON traffic crawled along Highway 26 as Gina and Ami navigated toward Beaverton. Strip malls and office parks replaced Portland's quirky neighborhoods. The clouds had settled in after the morning's rain, turning the suburban landscape into a study in grey.

"What's your take on the Daughters of Aradia?" Gina asked. "Are they really super fans—or just super creepy?"

Ami laughed. "Probably both. But if you're asking me whether they took Leigh, I don't think so."

"Really?"

"I know fandom can get intense, but kidnapping seems extreme."

"I don't know. People do crazy things when they're obsessed. Don't forget, I was right there when Tara was trying to slip something into Morgan's drink."

"A protection potion, she said."

"Right. Because witches are totally trustworthy when they're caught tampering with drinks."

The traffic thinned as they passed blocks of identical office parks. A sign for Washington Square Mall emerged through the mist.

"Take the next exit," Ami said, checking her phone. "Crafty Cloister isn't in the big mall—it's in one of those strip malls down the street."

They wound through a maze of parking lots until the craft store's faux-Gothic facade came into view. The orange and blue sign glowed against the pewter sky.

"How do you want to play this?" Ami asked.

"You hang back and let me take the lead," Gina said.

"You sure?"

"She might know who you are, but she definitely won't know me."

"What are you going to say?"

"Not sure yet. I'll play it by ear."

Through the wall of windows, Gina could see aisle after aisle of craft supplies stretching into the distance. A cardboard display near the entrance advertised "Fall into Savings!" with cutout leaves in harvest colors.

Gina strode into Crafty Cloister like she owned every glue gun and decorative button in the place. The fluorescent lights cast an unflattering glow on the aisles of seasonal décor and off-brand yarn.

"Customer service," she barked at a teenager arranging friendship bracelet threads.

He pointed toward a desk near the center of the store, where a gangly clerk in an orange polo was reorganizing coupon flyers.

"I need to see Robbie Jo Redding," Gina announced, channeling her own inner Karen. "Immediately."

The clerk's Adam's apple bobbed. "Um, may I ask who's—"

"Gina from Corporate." She managed to infuse the word 'corporate' with enough menace to make the clerk's eyes widen.

"Should I just…call her to come out here?"

"You could do that…" Gina leaned forward, reading his

name tag. "*Trevor*. But do you really want that to be the last thing you do before I terminate you?"

Trevor's face went the color of discount poster board. "I'll…I'll take you right back."

"Good choice."

He led her through a door marked "Employees Only," past bathrooms that smelled of artificial cinnamon, and into a warren of cramped offices. Cheerful signs about productivity and teamwork lined the hallway, their messages at odds with the soul-crushing beige walls.

"Second door on the left," Trevor whispered.

"Have a blessed day," Gina said with a smirk, enjoying how it made him scurry away faster.

She didn't bother knocking. Robbie Jo Redding sat behind a desk cluttered with vendor catalogs and safety meeting notices, her phone quickly disappearing from view as the door swung open. She was probably playing a game.

"Excuse me, who do you think you—" Robbie Jo began, her protest dying as Gina reached into her purse.

With theatrical slowness, Gina withdrew the black and red wig from her Stockdale's reusable grocery bag. She dropped the tangle of hair onto Robbie Jo's desk, right on top of a stack of purchase orders.

"Thought you might want this back," Gina said. "Though I have to say, the righteous protester look suits you better than wannabe goth spy."

Robbie Jo's face drained of color, but only for a second. Her jaw set in a line as rigid as her starched collar. "I've never seen that…that thing before in my life." She gestured at the wig as if it might bite. "And I don't appreciate strangers barging into my office making accusations."

"No? Maybe this will refresh your memory." Gina pulled up her phone and started swiping. "Here you are outside Powell's yesterday, leading the charge against satanic influence. Very passionate speech, by the way. Loved the bit about protecting our children's souls."

Robbie Jo's lips thinned. "I stand by every word."

"Oh, I'm sure you do. And here—" Gina swiped again, "—is someone at the gallery wearing the exact same Talbot's suit. Circa what, 2009? Though they've accessorized with this fetching wig, a grandma headscarf, and sunglasses big enough to hide behind. The police are very interested in this person, since they were last seen near where Morgan Mallory disappeared."

Robbie Jo got even paler. Her throat worked soundlessly for a moment. "I…I can explain."

"Of course you can." Gina moved forward, planting both hands on the desk. The wig slid sideways, revealing a Post-it note about ordering more seasonal ribbon. "And you're going to explain every last thing. Unless you'd prefer I share these lovely before-and-after shots with your devoted followers? I'm guessing all those MAGA moms from here to Newport Beach would love to know their fearless leader has been consorting with witches."

Robbie Jo drew a shaky breath. "Fine. Yes, I was at the gallery. But I wasn't there to do anything to Morgan Mallory."

"No? Just wanted to soak in some culture between protest shifts?"

"It's my daughter." Robbie Jo's voice cracked, her cheeks flushing deep red as she stared at her hands. "She loves those books." The last words came out as barely a whisper, like she was confessing a mortal sin.

Gina blinked. Of all the possible explanations, this wasn't one she'd expected. "Let me get this straight. The daughter of the Family Values Majority leader is a *Witch on the Train* fan?"

"Yes." Robbie Jo's shoulders slumped. "Chloe's a…" She glanced around the empty office before continuing in a mortified whisper, "…*Trainer*." She pulled a tissue from a box decorated with a Bible quote and dabbed her eyes, her face still burning with shame. "I was there to get an autograph for her. We haven't been…things are difficult between us right now. I thought if I could get her favorite author's signature… Obviously, I had to wear a disguise."

"Yes, obviously," Gina said. "Because otherwise people might think you were a hypocrite."

"Exactly!" Robbie Jo nodded vigorously, her complete lack of self-awareness almost impressive.

A hypocritical Family Values crusader, Gina thought. *Color me surprised.* "Did you end up meeting with Morgan?"

"No, I never got the chance."

"Did you see her leave?"

Robbie Jo shook her head. "I was waiting to approach her when that whole thing happened with the poisoned drink. If you ask me, those satanists are the ones responsible." Her righteous anger resurfaced. "Those Daughters of Aradia women are clearly dangerous. They're the ones you should be investigating."

"Duly noted. Go on."

"Once the police showed up, I…well, I slipped out the back and got rid of my disguise."

Gina studied her for a long moment. The woman was many things—self-righteous, hypocritical, oblivious—but she wasn't lying. "Okay, I believe you. We're done here."

"Really?"

"Really." Gina turned to leave, but Robbie Jo called after her.

"Wait! You won't tell anyone about this, will you?"

Gina paused in the doorway. "Not if you and your group leave the bookstores and libraries alone."

"Fine," Robbie Jo said, then added with a smug little smile, "But you can't suppress us. We're the majority now, you know."

Oh, I know, Gina thought as she walked away. *God help us all.*

GINA FOUND Ami waiting by the exit, scrolling through her phone with a worried expression. As they hurried to the car, Gina filled her in on Robbie Jo's confession.

"So she was just there for an autograph?" Ami sighed as they climbed in. "Another dead end. I hate to say it, but it's looking more and more like the Daughters are involved. Maybe we should go to the police, tell them Morgan's super-fans might have taken her."

"Not yet." Gina pulled out of the parking lot, navigating around a pothole. "The cops will want more evidence before they move on something like this. Accusing a group who's that active on social media without proof?" She clicked her tongue. "That could backfire big time. But I started to tell you earlier—there's a Daughters of Aradia meet-up tonight at some witchy apothecary in town. Crow-something. We'll confront Tara directly."

"I can't go."

"Sure you can. It's only dudes who are not allowed."

"No, you don't understand." Ami twisted her rings nervously. "These aren't just witches—they're *Trainers*. Morgan's superfans. I have to stay on their good side for busi-ness reasons. If I mess up that relationship…" She shrugged. "Best friend or not, Morgan would never forgive me. You're on your own with this one."

"Great." Gina drummed her fingers on the steering wheel. "Except they all saw me accuse their high priestess of drink-spiking. If I walk in there, they'll probably stone me on sight." She gave a hollow laugh. "Why did I give back that stupid wig?"

Ami sat up straight. "You can borrow one of Morgan's!"

"Morgan has wigs?"

"Of course she does. You think she has time for that high-maintenance hair? Her real hair is brown. She always travels with at least four wigs and tons of outfits." Ami gave Gina an appraising look. "You and Leigh are about the same size. We can get you the full disguise."

A little thrill ran through Gina—the same one she used to get playing dress-up as a kid. Back then, her mom's closet had been an endless source of alter egos. Now she was about to raid a bestselling author's wardrobe. *Focus,* she told herself. *This is about finding Morgan, not playing supernatural dress-up.*

But she couldn't quite suppress her grin.

chapter 11

· · ·

Witchcore Meets Whimsigoth

AFTER AN EARLY DINNER at Higgins (Berenstein's choice—"If we're playing detective, we deserve proper sustenance!"), Gina headed over to Ami's hotel. The butternut squash soup and local mushroom tart felt like lead in her stomach, anxiety mixing with anticipation.

Ami opened the door and immediately handed Gina a glass of wine. "Come on. We have work to do." She led Gina into one of the bedrooms, where a collection of wigs perched on elegant stands like avant-garde art pieces. One stand sat conspicuously empty, its bare dome an accusation. Gina's throat tightened. Somewhere in the Rose City, Morgan was missing, while Gina was about to play dress-up.

"This one." Ami lifted a wig in a deep auburn shade, the color of autumn leaves catching fire. "It's more understated than Morgan's signature red, but different enough from your own hair that no one will make the connection."

"I'm in your capable hands, maestro."

Gina followed Ami into the huge marble bathroom, where bottles and jars cluttered every counter. Perched atop the vanity like a furry gargoyle was Gertrude, her tail flicking back and forth as she watched them with unblinking green eyes.

"Does she always supervise your makeup routine?" Gina asked, setting her wine glass next to the sink.

Ami laughed. "She likes to be in the middle of everything. Plus, I think she enjoys the warmth from the vanity lights."

Gertrude let out a soft mew, as if confirming Ami's theory.

"Well, at least someone's enjoying this process." Gina picked up a deep burgundy lipstick, examining the label. "I feel like I'm about to guest star on *Drag Race*."

"Morgan never goes anywhere without her kit."

"It's a pretty serious kit."

Ami worked her magic with eyeliner and bobby pins, her running commentary getting more enthusiastic with each sip of wine. She nailed the perfect wing on the first try, but the false lashes were a whole other story. Gina's eyelids drooped under their weight as she tried to adjust. Gertrude seemed fascinated by Gina's changing appearance, tilting her head as if trying to reconcile this new version with the woman she'd met before.

"Stop blinking," Ami said, steadying Gina's chin with one hand. She wielded the lipstick—something dark and vampy —like a weapon. "I mean it."

"What exactly is the dress code for this coven meeting?" Gina asked, trying not to smudge her lipstick.

"The usual. Witchcore-meets-whimsigoth."

"I have no idea what that means. It sounds like something Berenstein would post on TikTok."

"Trust the process." Ami disappeared into the other room and returned with an armful of black fabric. "The Daughters take their aesthetic very seriously."

Gina slipped into the oversized black shirt, its intricate lace overlay like liquid shadow against her skin. The pleated skirt swished playfully around her calves. Ami topped off the ensemble with a tailored coat, its collar framing Gina's face like dark wings.

As Gina stood fully dressed in Morgan's clothes, Gertrude jumped down from her perch and wound between Gina's feet, leaving a trail of black fur on the borrowed witch wear.

"Thanks, kitty," Gina muttered. "Nothing says authentic witch like cat hair." Still, she couldn't help but smile as she bent to scratch behind Gertrude's ears, appreciating the feline stamp of approval.

"Final touches." Ami fastened a silver moon choker around Gina's neck before fetching a pair of chunky black boots. "Morgan wore these at her last signing in Vancouver. What size are you?"

"Eight, eight and a half."

"These are nine, but give them a try."

Gina laced up the boots, their silver hardware glinting. As she stood before the full-length mirror outside the bathroom, her breath caught. The auburn wig's loose waves softened her features, while dramatic eye makeup made her green eyes look huge and mysterious. She barely recognized herself.

"Okay, I'm so stealing this outfit," she joked, imagining herself strutting down Maidenwell's cobblestone streets. What would Frau Loneskum say if she saw Gina dressed like this? Imagining the matriarch's perfectly penciled eyebrows shooting up at the sight of her made Gina stifle a snort.

Ami stepped back, studying Gina with a critical eye, like an art curator appraising a new installation. "Perfect. Looks like you've made an effort, but not too much effort." She nodded, satisfied. "The Daughters will eat you up."

Gina flinched, her hand flying instinctively to her throat.

"Metaphorically speaking," Ami added quickly, noticing her reaction. She reached out and adjusted the choker with gentle fingers. "Deep breaths."

"So tell me what happens at these meet-ups," Gina said. "There won't be any blood rituals or—"

"God, no." Ami smiled. "Think more along the lines of wine and tarot readings. Heavy emphasis on the wine." She swirled her glass. "Morgan's done appearances at these things all over the country. It's mostly women who are into crystals, herbs, astrology—that whole scene. They'll probably spend half the night dissecting that snippet Morgan read from *Things That Go Bump Under the Covers.*"

"So it's a book club with better accessories?"

"Exactly." Ami's expression shifted. "But they'll definitely be talking about Morgan's disappearance. Keep your ears open."

The empty wig stand caught Gina's eye again, and she straightened her shoulders. Book club or coven, she had a job to do.

"Any special witch lingo I should know?" Gina asked, already mentally preparing herself for an evening of herb-clutching role play. At least there would be wine.

"Just say 'Merry meet, merry part, and merry meet again.'"

"That's kind of a mouthful. Merry what now?"

"On second thought, just nod a lot. And if anyone asks your moon sign, tell them."

"That's easy. Gemini."

"Makes sense." Ami's knowing smile made Gina wonder if there was some cosmic joke she wasn't getting. "Geminis love connecting the dots." She pressed a small velvet bag into Gina's hand. "Here—some crystals for authenticity. Clear quartz for clarity, amethyst for intuition. Rose quartz for—"

"Let me guess—love?" The word slipped out before she could stop it. Her mind wandered traitorously to Reeve. If these crystals actually worked…but no. Even if she had access to magical love rocks, would she really want to use them on him? Maybe she needed to use them on herself instead—clear out whatever emotional constipation kept her running from actual intimacy. God, she was really overthinking some random pieces of polished rock.

"Protection, actually." Ami's smile faded. "Just in case."

Gina slipped the velvet bag into her coat pocket, trying to ignore how the gentle clink of crystals sent an unexpected shiver down her spine. Although she loved the idea of supernatural stuff, the practical, cynical part of her brain wanted to dismiss this whole witchy business as New Age nonsense. But after that electric moment with Morgan at the reading…

As she turned toward the door, a strange shiver ran through her fingertips—probably just static electricity from the velvet.

But suddenly, the puzzle piece that had been floating around her brain since dinner snapped into focus with unsettling clarity. Her mouth went dry.

"You okay?" Ami asked, her brow furrowing with concern.

"Okay, this is going to sound crazy," she said, trying to shake off the weird certainty humming through her veins. "But did any of the Daughters try to contact Morgan before her visit?"

Ami pressed her lips together, considering. "Not that I can remember, but I can check her emails and texts. What exactly are you looking for?"

"I don't know. Warning signs? Sometimes superfans cross lines without realizing it."

"That's not a bad idea. I'll dig through her accounts."

"Thanks." Gina opened the door. "Wish me luck."

"Call me the second—and I mean the second—you leave that meeting." Ami's fingers twisted her rings. "Even if you don't learn anything."

"Promise." As Gina made her way to the elevator, the image of the empty wig stand lingered in her mind like a bad omen. She pushed the thought away. Time to put her new witchy persona to work.

THE CLOVER & Crow occupied a boxy old house with a wraparound porch supported by thick wooden posts. A stylized sign featured a woodcut of a crow clutching a sprig of clover in its beak. More Brooklyn hipster than Salem witch trials, that was for sure. Gina climbed the wooden steps, her boots clicking against the weathered boards.

Inside, the scent hit her first: dried herbs and something deeper, earthier—possibly patchouli, though she'd never admit to recognizing it. Polished wood floors and exposed brick walls somehow made the cluttered space look Instagram-ready.

Gina browsed around for a minute. Glass jars of herbs and crystals lined industrial-chic shelving, while leather-bound books on everything from astrology to Zen meditation filled floor-to-ceiling bookcases. A marble counter displayed handmade jewelry, each piece tagged with promises of energy and intention. In the center of the room, a farmhouse table held elaborate gift boxes wrapped in dried flowers and twine, featuring bundles of sage and tiny bottles of oil.

"You must be here for the meet-up." The clerk behind the counter smiled warmly—young, friendly, with an undercut that somehow worked with her cottagecore dress.

"And you must be psychic." The joke left Gina's lips before she could stop it.

The clerk laughed. "Just observant. It's upstairs in the event room." She gestured toward a staircase at the back of the store that looked steep enough to qualify as a leg day workout.

Thank god this event was women-only. Gina thought of Berenstein as she approached the stairs. Between his knees and these steps, he would have been cursing all the way up.

Echoes of Taylor Swift's latest breakup anthem grew

louder with each step. At the top, Gina paused in the doorway, looking into the event room and taking in the scene.

The warm glow of Edison bulbs and faux candles illuminated a dozen women rocking their witchy finest. A folding table near the window held an impressive spread of snacks—fancy cheese, raw veggies, and what looked like homemade chocolate truffles. Wine glasses sparkled everywhere, just as Ami had promised, their contents ranging from deep red to pale rosé. Some women stood in small groups, gesturing animatedly with their free hands, while others perched on metal folding chairs lining the walls. From the middle of the largest cluster, Tara Diaz commanded attention, her purple hair gleaming under the warm lights.

Gina took a deep breath and adjusted her borrowed coat, channeling every ounce of Morgan's mystique that she could muster. Then she glided into the room.

A short woman materialized at Gina's side like a friendly ghost, her black pixie cut framing a pretty heart-shaped face. "Welcome! I'm Cheryl, the resident newbie wrangler." She extended her hand.

"Uh…" Gina struggled to remember the phrase Ami had taught her. "Merry maids…?"

"Excuse me?"

"Sorry, I'm Lilly DuBois. Just in town for the weekend."

"Nice. Where are you from?"

"New York, originally. But I'm now living in Eastern Washington. Walla Walla."

"Quite the change! Wine country to wine country, though, right?" Cheryl's laugh tinkled like the shop's crystal wind chimes. "Speaking of which, red or white?"

"Red, please. When in doubt…"

"Good choice. We've got a lovely Pinot from Bethel Heights." Cheryl steered her toward the refreshment table. "So, what brings you to our little gathering?"

"I was in town for Morgan Mallory reading. Then I heard

what happened." Gina fingered the velvet bag of crystals in her pocket. "It kind of messed me up."

"Morgan's disappearance has shaken all of us." Cheryl's voice dropped. "That's partly why we're gathering tonight. Tara's planning a location ritual."

Perfect. Gina accepted a generously filled wine glass. "I just saw some posts on social about it. Do they have any leads?"

"Nothing concrete, but—" Cheryl glanced around conspiratorially. "Tara thinks there's more going on than the police understand. You know, given Morgan's…abilities."

Before Gina could probe further, the group began gravitating toward the circle of chairs. She found herself wedged between Cheryl and a woman wearing enough bangles to supply a Pier 1 going-out-of-business sale. The familiar rhythm of female friendship—even temporary and under false pretenses—felt comforting. It reminded her of late nights with Danielle and Susan in their Dartmouth dorm, plotting world domination over contraband wine and microwaved nachos.

Taylor Swift faded into something more ethereal—all wind chimes and pan flutes. Tara took center stage, her purple hair catching the light like a cosmic crown. "Sisters, welcome."

Her eyes swept the room, casual and warm, until they snagged on Gina's face. The warmth drained from Tara's expression. She kept staring, her dark-lined eyes narrowing to obsidian slits, and Gina's choker suddenly felt way too tight.

chapter 12

· · ·

The Circle Is Complete (But I'm Not)

JUST LIKE THAT, Tara's death stare clicked off as suddenly as a kid's Halloween flashlight.

Her face softened as she turned back to the group, though Gina's heart kept doing the cha-cha against her ribs. *Weird.*

"Tonight we gather in love and light, seeking to aid our missing sister Morgan," Tara intoned. She lit three white candles arranged in a triangle on the floor—real ones this time, their flames steady in the still air. Because nothing said "spiritual awakening" quite like violating the fire code in an old wooden building.

Sage smoke curled through the room as another woman moved in a slow circle with a smoldering bundle. Gina fought the urge to cough. Between the incense and her nerves, her throat felt like she'd chain-smoked her way through a Lilith Fair weekend.

"Join hands, sisters."

Cheryl's palm was warm against Gina's left hand. On her right, Pier 1 Chick's bangles jingled as their fingers interlocked. The circle of women swayed slightly, like seaweed caught in a gentle current.

"Morgan Mallory, we call to you." Tara's voice dropped an

octave, resonating in the quiet room. "Through the veil of shadow, through the mists of confusion, we send you our light. We are your beacon. We are your anchor."

The group repeated her words, their voices overlapping in an oddly haunting chorus. Despite herself, Gina felt goosebumps ripple up her arms. The air seemed to thicken, like a humid August afternoon in New York.

"By earth, by air, by fire, by water," Tara chanted.

A sharp crack split the silence—one of the candles had popped loudly, sending wax spattering across the hardwood floor. Several women gasped. Tara's eyes flickered to Gina again, this time with something that looked like genuine surprise.

Is this all part of the show? Gina squeezed her borrowed crystals through her coat pocket, trying to ground herself in reality. But reality felt increasingly subjective in this circle of believers, with their steady chanting and the unexplained electricity humming through her veins.

Tara closed her eyes, swaying slightly. "The energy flows strong tonight, sisters. I sense…water. Dark water. And stone beneath the city." Her voice took on an otherworldly quality that sent fresh chills down Gina's spine. "She walks in shadow, but her light still burns."

The candle flames flickered in perfect unison, as if caught in an unfelt breeze. Gina's skepticism warred with the undeniable sensation that something genuinely mysterious was happening. Either these women were incredible actors, or she'd stumbled into something far stranger than she'd bargained for.

"The circle is complete," Tara said finally, her voice returning to normal. "May the Goddess return Morgan to us." She opened her eyes, and for a brief moment, they seemed to glow with an inner fire that made Gina's breath catch in her throat.

After the candles were extinguished and the sage smoke

had mostly dissipated, the group's vibe shifted like a theater audience after the house lights come up. The wine loosened everyone up, turning the discussion into a mashup of book club and midnight conspiracy theories. Women shared their favorite Morgan passages, debated her disappearance, and argued about which crystals packed the most protective punch. Their genuine concern pulled Gina in, though she kept mentally cataloging every detail.

"The thing is," a redhead named J'ala said, swirling her rosé, "Morgan always claimed her books came from real experiences. What if someone wanted to silence her? Stop her from revealing too much about the Unseen World?"

Murmurs of agreement rippled through the circle. Gina caught Tara studying her hands, a slight frown creasing her forehead.

"Morgan's always been careful about what she reveals," Tara said, her voice oddly flat. "The real magic stays hidden between the lines."

Tara's tone set off all Gina's warning bells. She opened her mouth to probe further, but Cheryl was already pulling her toward the snack table, insisting she try the vegan chocolate truffles that someone's girlfriend had made.

"They're infused with rose quartz energy," Cheryl explained, as if that made them taste any less like chocolate-covered raspberries.

As the night wound down, Gina found herself actually reluctant to leave. These women might be deep in the woo-woo end of the pool, but their concern for Morgan felt genuine. Plus, she had a feeling Tara knew more than she was saying—assuming Gina could get her alone for five minutes without blowing her cover.

Most women filtered out in twos and threes, trailing clouds of patchouli and wine-warmed laughter. Gina lingered, gathering empty glasses with exaggerated helpfulness while watching Tara from the corner of her eye. The purple-haired woman moved through the space with surprising grace, extinguishing candles and gathering scattered crystals.

"Need a hand?" Gina asked, proud of how steady her voice sounded. "Least I can do after all that…spiritual energy sharing."

Tara's eyes narrowed slightly, but she nodded. "Sure. Wipe down the altar?"

They worked in silence for several minutes, the clink of glasses and rustle of cloth almost masking the tension. The questions bubbling in Gina's mind threatened to spill out all at once. Finally, she took a steadying breath.

"Can we talk about what happened at the gallery?" When Tara didn't respond, Gina pressed on. "The drink incident. I saw what you did, and I'd really like to understand why."

Tara's hands stilled on the velvet cloth she was folding. In the dimmed shop lights, her jewelry caught subtle gleams, like stars about to fall.

Neither spoke, the quiet growing thicker by the second.

"I would never hurt her," Tara finally said, her voice barely above a whisper. "That drink…it wasn't poison. Just moon water infused with lavender and rose petals. Basic protection magic." Her fingers twisted a silver ring anxiously. "I saw what was happening with that man, the way he was ruining everything."

"Emerson?"

Tara nodded. "I thought I could break whatever hold he has on her. Shield her somehow."

Something shifted in the air between them, thick with unspoken understanding. Tara's hands trembled as she smoothed the velvet cloth over and over, like she was trying to iron out more than just wrinkles.

"What exactly is he doing to her?" Gina asked, keeping her voice gentle. She recognized that mix of protectiveness and desperation—she'd felt it herself often enough with friends in bad relationships.

Tara's chin lifted defiantly. "He's trying to make her quit the series. Says it's beneath her." Her voice dripped with contempt. "But these books aren't just stories—they're doorways to truth. Real magic wrapped in fiction." A tear slipped down Tara's cheek. "Love, too. *Real* love."

"You're saying he wants her to—"

"He's making her deny who she really is! Everything that makes her special. Everything that makes her Morgan."

Gina watched Tara brush away the tear with the back of her hand, leaving a smudge of eyeliner like a bruise. The raw pain in her voice was impossible to fake.

"Look," Tara said, meeting Gina's eyes with surprising intensity. "I know how it looked at the gallery. But Morgan's books…they showed me who I could be. Who I really am. I'd never do anything to harm her." She laughed, a brittle sound. "Though I guess spiking her drink wasn't my brightest moment."

"No," Gina agreed. "Probably not the best plan."

A brief smile played across Tara's face. She turned away, gathering herb bundles with slightly trembling hands. The conversation was clearly over, but something fundamental had changed. The woman before her was no kidnapper—just someone who cared too much, too fiercely, about the wrong things.

Outside in Portland's damp night air, Gina's thoughts spun in every direction. If Tara was innocent, they were back to square one. But what she said about Emerson nagged at Gina's mind, refusing to settle. There was more to uncover there, buried beneath his polished Boston banker veneer.

Back in her hotel room, Gina kicked off her boots and collapsed onto the bed. The scent of sage clung to her clothes, oddly comforting. Who would have thought she'd end up spending her evening holding hands with strangers, chanting about protective crystals? And weirder still—she hadn't hated it.

The earnestness of those women stayed with her, their unshakeable belief in something bigger than themselves. When was the last time she'd felt that kind of connection? Even in Maidenwell, where she'd found friendship and purpose, there were always walls up, secrets kept.

She wondered if the village had its own version of the Daughters of Aradia tucked away somewhere. Knowing Maidenwell, probably. Maybe Millicent would know—though explaining why she was asking would be an interesting conversation.

Gina fished her phone from her pocket. She stared at the bright screen, hesitating. God, she'd forgotten to check in with Ami.

> Back safe. No hexes or curses. Though I might have accidentally joined a coven

Ami's response came instantly:

> Call me. Found something big

Gina's heart skipped. Sleep would have to wait—the mystery of Morgan's disappearance had just taken another turn. She hit the call button, pulling her knees to her chest.

When Ami answered, Gina said, "Hey. So Tara's clean—well, not clean-clean. She definitely spiked that drink. But she wasn't trying to hurt Morgan."

"What was she up to, then?"

"She's just…" Gina paused, choosing her words carefully.

"She's deeply invested in Morgan's…authenticity. And really not a fan of Emerson."

"I could have told you that."

"I think you actually did, but it was good to hear it from the horse's mouth."

"Speaking of unwanted admirers," Ami said, "I came across something weird in Morgan's old emails. Have you heard of Dean K. Forman?"

"Should I have?"

"He's another author—based here in Portland. He approached Morgan about six months ago. Proposed a collab on a series he was working on called *Sailing with the Sea Witch.* Offered her seventy-five percent of the profits just to put her name on the cover with his."

Gina sat up straighter. "I'm no expert, but that seems… generous. Too generous?"

"Gets better. When she said no, he bumped it to ninety percent. Morgan kept refusing, so he kept pushing. She ended up having to block him."

Something about that name tickled the edge of Gina's exhausted mind, but she couldn't quite grasp it. The events of the evening had left her mental filing cabinet in disarray. "Was he at the reading? The gallery opening?"

"Not on any guest lists," Ami said. "I'm going through social media photos now, and I'll check with Lauren tomorrow, see if she noticed anyone suspicious hanging around."

"Can we meet for coffee tomorrow?" Gina asked, stifling a yawn. "I need to process all this with actual caffeine in my system."

"Sure. The hotel here has an amazing breakfast. Nine-thirty?" There was a pause. "Unless that's too early after your night of witchcraft and wine?"

"I'll manage."

"Stay safe. And Gina? Thanks for doing all this."

After hanging up, Gina changed into her t-shirt and

crawled under the hotel's crisp sheets. But sleep, when it came, was anything but restful.

Her dreams were a bizarre kaleidoscope of the evening's events, twisted and transformed in weird new ways. The circle of women morphed, their faces blending together like watercolors. Tara's purple hair became a twilight sky. Candlelight flickered across high cheekbones and knowing smiles. Hands clasped, soft and warm, their touch electric against her skin.

Then the dream shifted and suddenly she was back in that circle, except now she and all the women were dancing. Not the awkward white-girl swaying she usually defaulted to at weddings—this was all flowing movements and bare feet and…oh. Someone's fingers were on her shoulders, trailing down her arms, sending shivers everywhere. She turned, expecting Cheryl or that redhead with her crystal-infused chocolate or maybe even Ami's kind face.

Instead—because dreams were the worst—she found herself staring into Reeve's intense grey eyes.

His touch lingered on her back even as his face hardened into that same accusing glare from their big fight. The ground beneath her feet turned to quicksand, pulling her down, down, down into an abyss of swirling colors and distant whispers.

Her eyes snapped open at 3 a.m..

Jesus. She kicked off the tangled sheets, but the dreams wouldn't let go. And here she'd been telling herself she was only interested in the witchy scene because of the case, but now she wasn't so sure. Maybe there was something else…

She pulled the pillow over her face and groaned. *Great.* Because this case wasn't complicated enough already.

chapter 13

· · ·

I Might Be Entering My Witch Era

THE MORNING SUN hit Gina's face like a rude awakening, scattering pieces of last night's dreams before she could pin them down. But her body remembered—the electric current of joined hands, the heady scent of sage, and…she pushed away the memory of Dream-Reeve's fingers trailing down her spine. *Nope. Not going there.* She had a missing author to find and mysterious emails to investigate. No time for romantic ghost stories, especially ones starring emotionally unavailable security officers who wouldn't even text her back.

She gathered Morgan's borrowed clothes—the black dress, coat, jewelry, and boots—arranging them into a Heathman's plastic laundry bag. The wig went in last, its auburn strands tangled from the evening's activities.

Down in the lobby, she found Berenstein nose deep in *The Oregonian.*

"Ready for breakfast?" she asked, trying to sound more awake than she felt.

"I googled the restaurant," Berenstein said, practically vibrating with excitement. "The Urban Farmer. Get this—they've got their own rooftop bees making honey. And the coffee's supposed to be exceptional. *Hacienda La Esmeralda Gesha*. From a small farm in Panama which only produces 1.8 tons of beans a year." His eyes lit up. "Though I wouldn't say no to a good bagel too."

"You had me at coffee," Gina said as they pushed through the front doors. "After last night, I'm going to need about three cups."

As they walked, she caught her reflection in a boutique window and winced at her mascara-smudged eyes and hair that looked like she'd styled it with a leaf blower. It was the Universe's way of saying maybe skip the fourth glass of Pinot next time you're undercover at a witch meeting.

"So," Berenstein said, "how was your evening with the Daughters? Did you solve any mysteries? Cast any spells? Turn anyone into a newt?"

"It was actually…" Gina paused, searching for the right words. "Kind of amazing?"

"Oh?"

"I've never been much for group activities," Gina admitted. "When I was young, especially. I was always more of a… stand in the corner and judge people kind of girl." She remembered how she hated it when her college roommate dragged her to all the Sigma Delt rush parties.

"But this was different. These women, they just…" Her hands moved in the air, trying to capture the indescribable something from last night. "They accepted everyone exactly as they were. No judgment, no pretense. Just…" She trailed off again.

Berenstein smiled at her. "Good for you, Biletti."

"Don't laugh," she said finally, "but…I kind of got into it. The whole vibe, I mean." She risked a glance at him. "I might be entering my Witch Era."

The words hung in the air between them, and Gina felt her cheeks warm. God, she sounded like one of those Instagram influencers hawking crystal-infused water bottles. But there was no denying the pull she'd felt in that circle, the way the energy had sparked and swirled around them all like invisible lightning.

Instead of the teasing she expected, Berenstein's face softened with understanding. "You know what I've learned in my nearly seventy years on this earth?" He adjusted his thick glasses. "It's always good to open yourself up to new things. Worst comes to worst, you get a good story out of it. But you might discover a thing or two about yourself. Might even surprise yourself."

The wisdom in his words settled over her like a warm blanket. Trust Berenstein to drop the perfect wisdom bomb, even if he did sometimes sound like he was auditioning for a self-help podcast.

Her mind drifted back to those crazy dreams from last night—the dancing…the feminine energy. And then Reeve's appearance. She wasn't sure what to make of any of it. But if anyone would understand complicated feelings, it would be Berenstein. He'd walked his own winding path to self-discovery long before she'd known him.

Sunlight flooded The Nines' atrium, bouncing off glass and greenery like some fancy greenhouse.

They found the restaurant tucked behind the front desk. Ami had already claimed a booth and was waving them over. Today she wore loose linen pants and a faded vintage Heathers t-shirt.

"Here," Gina said, passing over the Heathman's laundry bag. "Sorry about the sage smell. Those Daughters are serious about their smudging."

Ami waved away the apology. "I see you brought reinforcements," she said, smiling at Berenstein.

Berenstein, obviously making an effort to act casual,

extended his hand. "Larry Berenstein," he said. "We met at the gallery. I run a bookshop in—" He caught himself. "Well, let's just say I'm a huge fan of Morgan's work. The way she subverts small-town gothic tropes and how she uses magic as a metaphor for authenticity..." He trailed off, seemingly realizing he was gushing.

Gina jumped in to rescue him. "Berenstein knows a lot of authors. Maybe he could help us find this guy."

Ami nodded at Berenstein. "How much did Gina tell you?"

Before he could launch into full fanboy mode, Gina kicked him under the table. "Nothing about what you found last night," she said.

"Right." Ami leaned forward. "Six months ago, this author named Dean K. Forman starts emailing Morgan. Wants her to co-author a book with him—something called *Sailing with the Sea Witch*. Offered her seventy-five percent of the royalties just to put her name on the cover."

"Intriguing," Berenstein said, his earlier nervousness forgotten.

"Gets better. When she said no, he bumped it to ninety. Kept pushing until she had to block him."

"Did you know about this when it was happening?" Gina asked.

Ami shrugged. "Vaguely. There are tons of people who want a piece of the Morgan Mallory business. This seemed like something she was handling." She paused. "I should have paid more attention."

A waiter appeared with a steaming carafe of coffee. Berenstein's face fell slightly when he learned they didn't serve bagels, but he recovered quickly. "The Dungeness crab omelet, please. And some of that rooftop honey you're famous for."

"Just oatmeal for me," Gina said. "Plain." The thought of anything else made her queasy.

"Same," Ami said.

After the waiter left, Berenstein stirred his coffee thoughtfully. "So, you think this chap had something to do with Morgan's disappearance?"

"He's in Portland," Gina said. "And apparently had a beef with her."

"He wasn't on any guest lists," Ami said, pulling out her laptop. "No mentions on social media either. I tried looking him up—he's got a few books listed on some websites, but no author photos, no social presence. I found a link to his website on Goodreads, but the site's dead. It's like he barely exists."

Gina tapped her recently-black nails against the table's polished surface, a habit that used to drive Erik crazy. "Hey, can I borrow that for a sec?"

Ami slid the laptop across the table. "Knock yourself out."

"What are you looking for?" Berenstein leaned in, nearly tipping over his coffee cup in the process.

"Ever hear of the Wayback Machine?" Gina's fingers danced across the keyboard with the muscle memory of a thousand late-night research binges. "It's like Google meets time travel. Shows you websites that don't exist anymore— but have been archived."

The ancient loading bar crept across the screen. "Come on, come on," she muttered. A decade of cached web history populated the screen. "And…jackpot."

"What did you find?" Ami's spoon clattered against her bowl.

Gina spun the laptop around. "Meet Dean K. Forman, from like ten years ago."

Berenstein's thick glasses fogged up as he huffed at the screen. "But that's—"

"Frank DeMano," Ami finished. "The gallery owner."

"The guy who conveniently disappeared to Miami right after Morgan vanished." Gina sat back, a familiar surge of adrenaline coursing through her veins. This was it—the thread that would unravel everything. "Looks like someone's been playing a long game."

The coffee sat forgotten as they stared at the photo. A younger Frank smiled back at them, wearing the same pretentious wire-rimmed glasses and sporting a goatee that screamed 'aspiring writer trying too hard.'

"We need to take this to the police," Ami said, already reaching for her phone.

Gina opened her mouth to agree when the memory hit her. "Wait. Those boxes in the gallery's back room. Dean K. Forman—that's where I saw the name." Her fingers attacked the keyboard, navigating to a page of Dean's books. "It was some book called…here. *Shanghai Revenge.* Listen to this description."

She cleared her throat and read: "*A thrilling historical adventure set in the 1850s clipper ship era. When young Jack Briggs is forcibly shanghaied from the streets of Portland, Oregon—*"

"Jumpin' Jehoshaphat!" Berenstein's coffee cup froze halfway to his mouth. "The Shanghai tunnels!"

"The what now?" Gina looked up from the screen.

"Underground passageways beneath Old Town here in Portland. Back in the 1800s, they used them to move cargo from the waterfront." He paused, adjusting his glasses. "And sometimes to kidnap men for forced labor on ships. They'd drug them in bars, then haul them through the tunnels straight onto waiting ships."

"Oh hell no." Underground tunnels were definitely not in her job description. "Are these tunnels…still down there?"

"Some are. Most got sealed up, but…" His face lit up like a history professor who'd just discovered a lost civilization. "The gallery building looked extremely old. I wonder…"

"Call Dee," Gina said, already grabbing her bag. "The landlady. Tell her it's an emergency."

Twenty minutes later, Gina stood in the alley behind the DeMano Gallery, watching Dee Lokumbe sort through her massive ring of keys. September in Portland had turned surprisingly warm, and sweat prickled at the back of her neck as they waited.

"I don't like this," Dee said, testing another key in the lock. "Frank's pretentious, sure, but kidnapping?"

"Look at the evidence." Gina shifted her weight, already regretting her choice of shoes for what was turning into a very active morning. "The guy literally wrote a book about kidnapping people through underground tunnels. Then a famous author disappears from his gallery after rejecting his desperate attempts to collaborate?"

"It's true," Ami said. "About the collaboration, I mean."

"And the tunnels," Berenstein said. "They must run through here."

Dee worked another key into the stubborn lock. "Sure. The Shanghai tunnels are real enough—anyone who's lived in Portland knows about them. But any access points in this building were sealed up decades ago."

"Could we at least check?" Ami asked, her usual cool demeanor cracking slightly. "Please?"

"Fine." The key finally turned with a satisfying click. "But only because I need to, uh, document a possible leak in the basement anyway." She shot them a look that said she knew exactly what game they were playing.

The service entrance opened into a narrow hallway that still smelled of stale food and wine from the party. Their footsteps echoed against concrete floors as Dee led them through a maze of storage rooms cluttered with bubble wrap and empty frames.

"The basement is this way," she said.

A metal spiral staircase descended into darkness, its steps

so tight that Berenstein had to turn sideways to navigate them.

"I don't mean to be a Negative Nelly," he whispered, gripping the railing, "but how exactly would Frank manage to drag a woman down these stairs without anyone noticing?"

"You know," Gina paused on the steps to give Berenstein the side eye, "it's slightly disturbing that you have such a comprehensive knowledge of dragging women into basements."

"Oh, pshaw!"

The basement lights flickered to life with a buzz, revealing a low, cramped space. It smelled of wood shavings, old cardboard, and that particular musty dampness that seemed to haunt every basement Gina had ever been in.

Giant wooden picture frames lined the brick walls like abandoned doorways to nowhere. Tools were scattered across a workbench—box cutters, hammers, and what looked like an expensive mat cutter gathering dust. In one corner, a damaged canvas of geometric shapes lay propped against several gigantic wooden shipping crates.

And everywhere—stacked in corners, shoved under tables—were boxes of books marked "OVERSTOCK RETURN."

"Well," Gina said, picking up a book and flipping through its pages, "I think we've found Portland's least successful author."

"No wonder he was so desperate to partner with Morgan." Ami ran a finger along a box, leaving a trail in the dust. "This is depressing."

They spread out, searching behind boxes and tapping walls for hollow spots like they were in some kind of amateur detective movie.

Gina investigated each corner, mentally repeating her new mantra: *spiders are more afraid of you than you are of them* (a total lie her therapist suggested, but whatever got her through this basement reconnaissance mission).

But after fifteen minutes of searching, they'd found nothing but more dust, more books, and what appeared to be Frank's abandoned attempt at erotic pottery.

"Eww." Ami recoiled from what might have been an abstract ceramic rocket ship but probably wasn't.

"This is pointless," Gina said finally. "If there was a tunnel access down here, we would have found it by now."

"I told you," Dee said. "Those doorways to the tunnels were closed up during the renovation in the eighties."

"Maybe we should check upstairs again," Ami suggested. "The gallery itself might have something we missed."

Berenstein sneezed violently, sending up a cloud of dust. "I second that motion. This basement is trying to kill me."

As they climbed back up the narrow stairs, Gina couldn't shake the feeling they were missing something obvious. But what?

chapter 14

. . .

Into the Web

BACK IN THE gallery's main space, Gina rubbed her temples, trying to organize her scattered thoughts. Something about that night kept nagging at her, like a word stuck on the tip of her tongue.

"Dee," she said suddenly. "The security cameras—there was one near the bathroom the night Morgan disappeared. Pointed right at the door."

Dee's brow furrowed. "The interior cameras are all Frank's setup. I just maintain the ones outside."

"Can you show me where you saw it?" Ami asked.

Gina led them toward the back of the gallery. The bathroom was hidden at the end of a dim hallway that smelled of dust and cardboard. But when they reached it, Gina stopped short.

"That's not right." The camera that had been trained on the bathroom door now pointed in the opposite direction—towards one of the gallery chambers. "I swear it was aimed this way the night of the party. I specifically remember thinking it was weird."

Berenstein appeared behind them, phone in hand. "Hey,

look at this—I found something called the Portland Under-ground Tour. Starts at a pizza joint just a few blocks away."

"Oh yeah," Dee said, leaning against the wall. "I did that tour once. It's just the restaurant's basement complex. No real access to any tunnels."

But Gina barely heard them. Her attention was fixed on the massive painting dominating the hallway wall—a sailing ship caught in stormy seas, its dark wooden frame as wide as her hand. Something about it tugged at her memory. She stepped closer, studying the thick brushstrokes of waves against the ship's hull—

The world tilted sideways.

One second she was standing, the next her knees went rubbery, and the hallway swooped like she'd just stepped off a carnival ride. Her hand shot out, grabbing for anything solid, and connected with the frame of the painting.

The frame moved. Not to the side, but away from the wall.

"Whoa, steady there, missy." Berenstein caught her elbow as she stumbled. "Did that painting just—"

"Open?" Gina's head was still spinning, but she hadn't imagined it. Hidden hinges ran down one side of the heavy frame, allowing the whole thing to pivot outward. As Berenstein helped her pull it wider, they both froze at what lay behind it.

Set into the wall was an ancient dumbwaiter, its metal cage streaked with rust and decades of dust.

"Well," Gina said faintly, "I guess we found our access point."

Dee stepped closer to examine the dumbwaiter, running her fingers along the rusty metal frame. "I had no idea this was here. How did Frank even find it?"

Gina squinted at the wall, waiting for the room to stop spinning. "Look at the brickwork around the opening." She traced the uneven edges where newer mortar met old. "Someone sealed this up ages ago. Frank must have found it when he was renovating. Or trying to hang art." She pressed a hand against the wall to steady herself.

"Are you okay?" Ami touched her arm. "You went pretty pale there for a minute."

"I'm fine. Just got dizzy for a second." Which was weird, because Gina didn't do dizzy. Motion sickness, sure. Hangover vertigo, absolutely. But random swooning in art galleries? Not her thing.

Dee pulled out her phone and switched on the flashlight. "There's something down there." She aimed the beam into the shaft. "Looks like the car is still intact." She yanked experimentally on the thick rope that disappeared into the darkness. A mechanical ratcheting echoed up the shaft as the car slowly rose. It was about a yard on each side. Definitely big enough to hold a body.

"This doesn't make sense," Berenstein said. "We were just in the basement. There wasn't any sign of where this thing comes out."

"Unless..." The words came out of Gina's mouth before she could stop them, like someone else was doing the talking. "Unless it goes somewhere else." She grabbed the rope. "Lower me down."

"Are you insane?" Dee's eyes went wide. "That thing looks about as stable as my first marriage. The insurance liability—"

"It's only fifteen feet or so." Gina was already climbing into the metal car, ignoring the voice in her head screaming about tetanus shots. "What's the worst that could happen?"

"Do you want that alphabetically or in order of likelihood?" Berenstein asked.

But Gina had already wedged herself into the cramped space, her foot bumping against something in the corner. She reached down, fingers brushing against what felt like leather, cold and stiff. Holding it up to the beam of Dee's phone light, she frowned. "It's a bracelet."

The leather had been woven into intricate Celtic-style knots, with fine silver wire threaded through the pattern like metallic veins.

Ami gasped. "Oh god. That's Morgan's. I gave it to her last Christmas." Her voice cracked slightly. "The knots were supposed to be wards of protection."

"Yeah." Gina handed the bracelet to Ami. "Guess they didn't do their job." She looked up at the worried faces peering down at her. "Okay, folks. Time to see where this rabbit hole goes."

Metal groaned against metal as they lowered her into the gloom. The beam of her phone's flashlight caught flakes of rust drifting through the air like evil confetti. Each breath tasted of mold and decay and something else—something older and hungrier.

The shaft walls pressed in closer than she'd expected. Way closer. Like being lowered into a brick coffin. Not that she was claustrophobic—she'd always been fine in elevators and crowded subway cars. But this? This was different. Her chest tightened with each creaking descent.

Just when the urge to scream bubbled up in her throat, the car bumped against something solid.

"I'm at the bottom!" Her voice echoed weirdly off the ancient walls. "Go down to the basement—I'll try to find where this comes out."

The phone's flashlight caught something that wasn't brick—a wooden door set into the shaft wall. It swung open with a touch, showering her with dust. Gina twisted herself out of the car, breathing through her mouth to avoid the smell of decay as she crawled through the opening.

She emerged into what had probably started life as a storage closet back when Portland was still just a twinkle in some pioneer's eye. Now it was a nightmare of cobwebs—thick, dusty curtains of them hanging from ceiling to floor.

They brushed against her face, caught in her hair, wrapped around her arms like ghost fingers.

Oh god. Oh god oh god oh god.

Her throat seized up. She couldn't move. Couldn't breathe. The webs were everywhere, which meant the spiders were everywhere, and any second now one would drop onto her neck or crawl across her face or—

"Hello?" Her voice came out strangled. "Can anyone hear me?"

Muffled voices drifted from somewhere ahead. She called out again, louder this time, focusing on the sound of distant footsteps rather than the feeling of the dusty, feathery strands against her skin.

There—another door on the far wall. She lurched toward it, desperate to escape the web-draped tomb. But when she pushed against the weathered wood, it barely budged.

No no no no no.

The walls seemed to contract around her as panic clawed at her chest. She was going to die here, wrapped in century-old cobwebs like some kind of discount mummy, all because she couldn't pass up playing Nancy Drew—

The door shifted under her palm—just a fraction of an inch, but enough to spark a desperate hope through her spider-induced paralysis. She threw her shoulder against it, feeling the wood flex.

"Help!" The word ripped from her throat, high and terrified.

chapter 15

· · ·

Uté Lehman Pumps, Size 9

THE DOOR suddenly jerked open with a screech of rusted hinges, and hands grabbed Gina's arms, pulling her into blessed, cobweb-free space. She stumbled forward, collapsing against Ami, her whole body trembling like she'd just run a marathon.

"It's okay, it's okay." Ami's voice was steady and warm against her ear. "We've got you. You're safe."

"We heard you calling," Berenstein explained. "Came down the basement stairs and followed your voice. That shipping crate against the wall? Turns out it's actually a door."

Gina focused on breathing, on the solid feel of Ami's arms around her, on the blessed absence of anything with eight legs. When her heart finally downshifted from coked-out hummingbird to merely terrified rabbit, she straightened up and smacked Berenstein's arm. Hard.

"Ow! What was that for?"

"What kind of friend lets someone climb into a rusty death trap from the previous century?" Her voice was still shaky, but the anger helped push back the lingering panic. "Next time I suggest something that monumentally stupid, you're contractually obligated to stop me. I don't care if you have to sit on me."

"Noted." He rubbed his arm. "Though in my defense, you were already halfway in before any of us could object."

Gina pressed her palms against her eyes, trying to make the pieces fit together. "So Frank used the dumbwaiter to get Morgan down here, into this hidden room behind the fake crate. But then what? Where did they—"

"Look." Dee's voice echoed from the cobwebbed closet they'd pulled Gina from. "There's more."

They followed the beam of Dee's flashlight to where the closet's side wall opened into a narrow passage. The tunnel stretched before them like a throat, barely four feet across, its centuries-old brick walls sweating in the glow of their flashlights. A cool draft carried the smell of dankness and secrets.

"Holy mackerel," Berenstein breathed. "A genuine Shanghai tunnel."

"Hold up." Ami had detached herself from Gina's death grip and crouched down, phone light illuminating the packed earth floor. "These footprints…"

Two distinct sets of prints marked the packed dirt, both from dress shoes. Gina studied the pattern. One set was clearly larger—a man's dress shoe. But it was the other set that made her pulse quicken.

"Those are from a woman's shoe," she said, crouching down beside Ami. "See the smaller heel mark? Definitely pumps."

Dee knelt beside them, squinting. "Could be anyone's—"

"No," Ami cut in, her voice tight with recognition. "Those are Morgan's Uté Lehmans. The little kitten heel leaves that specific impression—Morgan was wearing them at the gallery. I remember because she complained they were pinching."

The confirmation sent a chill down Gina's spine. Morgan had walked this path, probably against her will, those designer pumps leaving delicate traces like clues in the dirt. Without hesitation, Gina took a step toward the tunnel's mouth. "We need to follow—"

"Absolutely not." Dee's voice carried the stern authority of someone who'd dealt with enough liability issues for one lifetime. "These tunnels were sealed off for a reason. They're over a century old and about as structurally sound as—"

"But Morgan is there somewhere," Gina said. "I know it."

"You're right. It definitely looks that way." Dee stood, brushing dirt from her knees. "We call the police. Let them handle it. I'm not having anyone else disappear down here."

"I agree. Enough heroics for one day, my dear." Berenstein's hand landed on Gina's shoulder. "Besides, we know where it leads. Shanghai tunnels only had one purpose—getting victims to the water."

Dee nodded. "The river's two blocks east. That's where they'd emerge."

Gina stared into the inky blackness, fighting the urge to charge ahead anyway. The tunnel seemed to breathe, its dank air carrying whispers of old crimes and fresh ones. But the memory of those cobwebs still crawled across her skin, and even her stubbornness had limits.

Usually.

Most of the time.

Sometimes.

OFFICER BANWO PICKED up on the first ring, his initial skepticism dissolving as Ami detailed their discoveries. His deep voice carried through the speaker: "Don't touch anything else. We'll be there in ten to take your statements."

Ten turned into forty-five minutes of watching uniformed officers string crime scene tape across the gallery entrance.

Gina's fingers kept brushing Morgan's bracelet, tracing

the intricate Celtic knots. She had convinced Ami to hold on to it for a little bit rather than surrendering it immediately. Let the cops have their precious chain of custody—sometimes talismans mattered more than evidence.

The afternoon dissolved into a blur of repeated statements and uncomfortable folding chairs. A detective from Missing Persons showed up—looking exactly like every true crime detective Gina had ever seen on Netflix—right down to the carefully neutral expression that somehow managed to radiate both sympathy and suspicion. Her name was Detective Talliere and she methodically extracted every detail about Frank's secret identity as Dean K. Forman, his pile of unsold books moldering in the basement, and all those pushy emails begging Morgan to "collaborate" on his next masterpiece.

"And you're certain about the shoe prints?" Detective Talliere asked for the third time, pen hovering over her notepad.

"Unless Frank has a previously undisclosed fondness for kitten heels, those prints belong to Morgan." The words came out sharper than Gina intended, but hours of repeating herself had worn her patience thin. She forced herself to take a steadying breath. "They're Uté Lehman pumps, size nine—the exact ones Morgan wore to the gallery. Ami confirmed it."

Detective Talliere's pen scratched against paper, recording another detail that would hopefully lead somewhere. The sound grated against Gina's already frayed nerves like fingernails on a chalkboard. She shifted in the metal folding chair, trying to find a position that didn't make her tailbone scream.

By seven, even Berenstein's endless supply of Morgan Mallory trivia had run dry. Detective Talliere finally released them with the usual warnings about remaining available for questions. Outside the gallery windows, Portland was showing off with a sunset straight out of a tourism brochure—all pink clouds and golden light that had no business being so pretty when Morgan was still missing.

Ami caught Gina in a quick hug that wrapped her in the scent of fancy soap. "I'll text the second I hear anything. Try to sleep?"

"Oh sure, because nothing says sweet dreams like almost becoming Spider-Queen of the Underground."

Back in her hotel room, she peeled off clothes that still carried traces of century-old dust. The shower helped, sort of. Hot water sluiced away the physical grime but did jack-all for the sensation of those webs brushing her face, that moment of pure terror when she thought she was trapped. Room service delivered some fancy mushroom risotto that she picked at while watching Portland light up like a Christmas tree.

Her phone buzzed—Berenstein, sending a string of witch emojis followed by "Proud of you today, kiddo." She started to type a snarky response about him failing in his anti-stupidity duties, but exhaustion made her fingers clumsy. The phone slipped from her grasp as the day's adrenaline crash finally caught up with her.

She needed sleep big time. But every time her eyes drifted shut, that tunnel stretched out in her mind. Morgan was down there somewhere—scared, trapped, maybe hurt. And here was Gina, letting Detective By-The-Book handle things while the clock kept ticking.

Her last coherent thought before exhaustion won was that maybe Morgan had been right. Maybe Gina was supposed to save her. And maybe she was completely screwing it up by lying here in a fancy hotel while Morgan waited in the dark.

SUNLIGHT PIERCED through the curtains Gina had forgotten to close. She dressed on autopilot—yesterday's jeans, clean shirt, hair pulled back without bothering to check the mirror. The streets were oddly empty as she walked to The Nines.

When Gina reached Ami's floor, an eerie silence hung in

the hallway, broken only by the distant hum of ice machines. The door to Ami's suite stood slightly open, which struck Gina as odd. There was no cart, no sign of housekeeping.

"Ami?" Gina called out, her voice barely above a whisper. Laughter drifted from deeper within the suite, soft and intimate.

She stepped inside, noting the scattered evidence of Ami's temporary residence—laptop on the coffee table, designer suitcase spilling dark blouses, empty wine glasses. But no Gertrude.

The bedroom door beckoned, not fully closed, a sliver of light spilling through the gap. Sounds emanated from within, breathy and intense, sending a shiver down Gina's spine. Every instinct told her to back away, to call out once more and flee before she discovered something she couldn't unsee.

Yet, as if pulled by an invisible force, she found herself drawn forward, heart pounding in her ears as she peered through the opening.

The sight that greeted her knocked the breath from her lungs.

Ami straddled Emerson on the massive bed, eyes closed and head thrown back as she rocked against him. Her perfect curves were gilded by morning light. His rower's muscles flexed beneath her.

Even as her mind reeled, unable to comprehend the betrayal unfolding before her eyes, she couldn't tear herself away. Heat bloomed low in Gina's belly as she watched the two people Morgan trusted most in the world, lost in the throes of forbidden passion.

How could they do this?

But at that moment, as if sensing her presence, Ami's eyes fluttered open, locking with Gina's. Emerson's gaze followed, his expression hungry and pleased.

"Now you know," Ami said softly, voice thick with satisfaction.

Understanding crashed through Gina's mind like a bucket of ice water. The secret emails from Dean sent through Ami's laptop. The staged Miami story that only Ami had confirmed. The bracelet placed too perfectly in the dumbwaiter. It had never been about Frank at all.

She turned and fled, her footsteps echoing in the hollow hallway as she ran from the sordid truth. Tears blurred her vision as she raced toward the elevator. She had to find Morgan, to break the news that would shatter her world and leave nothing but pain in its wake.

chapter 16

. . .

Where the Hell Did That Come From?

GINA WOKE WITH A START, heart racing, and sheets tangled around her legs. The darkness pressed in, thick and unfamiliar. Nothing made sense—not the angular shadows crawling across the ceiling, not the faint hum of unfamiliar traffic filtering through the window, not even the too-soft mattress beneath her.

As her eyes adjusted to the gloom, the contours of the room began to take shape. The photos of Portland's historic bridges on the walls, the suitcase propped against the dresser, the sweater she'd draped over the back of the chair before crawling into bed. Slowly, the fog of sleep began to dissipate, and recognition dawned.

She was in her room at the Heathman, exactly where she was supposed to be.

But something nagged at the edges of her consciousness. The vision clung to her—all heated flesh and wandering hands and...oh god. Emerson. And Ami. Together. Her stomach did a complicated gymnastics routine as the images flashed through her mind with HD clarity.

It was just a dream. Just a completely inappropriate, never-to-be-mentioned-to-anyone-ever dream.

She glanced at the alarm clock on the nightstand. 6:47 a.m. Too early to be awake, but too late to try and fall back asleep. But she needed to move, to do something to shake off the lingering unease.

With a groan, Gina forced herself out of her bed and into the bathroom. She needed a shower. A very cold one, though she'd rather die than admit why. Her twisted brain kept serving up a highlight reel of the dream: Emerson's taut, muscled shoulders, Ami's perfect curves.

The bathroom mirror didn't pull any punches. Her reflection stared back, hair wild, cheeks flushed, eyes a little too bright. Maybe this was what happened when your dry spell lasted longer than some people's marriages.

She snorted, wondering if she could expense a male escort under "preventative healthcare." The mental image of Peyton's face as she reviewed that particular reimbursement form almost made up for the mortification of the dream.

Almost.

Gina let the steaming water beat against her shoulders, praying the scalding heat would scour away the crazy. But even as she robotically soaped up, she kept picturing Ami and Emerson. *Could they…? No!*

In the stark light of day, her dream-induced suspicions about Ami seemed completely ridiculous. Dean K. Forman's existence was well-documented—by boxes and boxes of his failed literary ambitions. Morgan's bracelet had been in the dumbwaiter's ancient basket locked behind a secret painting —no way could Ami have planted it so perfectly. And the very idea of Ami and Emerson carrying on some secret affair while orchestrating Morgan's disappearance? Pure paranoid fantasy. Or the plot of a Lifetime movie.

"Just admit it, Biletti." Her voice echoed off the bathroom tiles as she scrubbed her face with a washcloth. "You're stressed, sleep-deprived, and have been making terrible life choices about dumbwaiters recently."

Water dripped onto the carpet as she padded across the room, clutching the too-small hotel towel around herself. She eyed the coffee maker lurking in the corner, the one she'd sworn never to use after that exposé about hotel room bacteria she'd read on a flight. But desperate times called for desperate measures. She needed caffeine more than she needed to maintain her germaphobe standards.

As the well-used machine gurgled and steamed, she tried to force herself to focus on the actual case instead of her subconscious's soft-core film festival.

But something about Ami's smile in the dream still haunted her.

The coffee maker wheezed out its last drops as Gina's phone buzzed. Her heart flipped a little bit when she saw a string of text messages crowding her screen from the lady herself.

> Hey, you up? Lots happening already

> Detectives been working all night going thru reports. Getting structural engineers to check those tunnels today. Still freaked about you going down there tbh

> Gave them L's laptop + passwords for forensics. Been making lists of everyone she's talked to lately. Agent's involved now too - they're digging thru all her emails etc

This was the real Ami—professional, focused, exhausted with concern for her best friend. Not the seductress from that twisted dream.

Gina shot back a quick text:

> Up and functioning. Sort of. Can head over if you want company?

The response came immediately:

Yes please! On my 3rd coffee. Gertrude's
giving me death glares for all the pacing &
muttering

After sending Berenstein a quick update (*Following up w/Ami. Will keep you posted. Get those knees some rest*), Gina grabbed her bag and headed out.

The Portland morning had dawned grey but dry, perfect weather for both brooding and investigating disappearances. She made a quick Starbucks pit stop, where her triple soy latte came with a bonus flirty smile from the barista. *Yeah, where were you last night, dude?*

She added two orders of egg bites to her purchase, knowing from personal experience how investigation-brain could make you forget about basic needs like food.

The Nines' hallway stretched out in elegant cream and blue, making Gina deeply aware of her slightly damp hair and thrown-together appearance. She checked Ami's door—properly closed and locked, thank god. Her dream-addled brain could shut up about secret trysts now.

Her knock was answered by Ami's voice, raised in what was clearly a police conversation: "Yes, Detective. I understand. We'll be here waiting."

Ami waved her in while wrapping up the call. She looked like she'd been awake for days, wearing a faded Red Sox t-shirt and yoga pants. Gertrude sat perched on a side table, green eyes narrowed in feline judgment.

"Breakfast," Gina announced, holding up the paper bag. "Because I'm betting 'third coffee' didn't come with actual food."

"You're an angel." Ami grabbed an egg bite. "Portland

PD's been coordinating with Miami police all morning. They're checking hotels, following up on that supposed 'business trip' excuse Frank gave everyone. So far nothing."

Gina's eyes guiltily scanned the suite for signs of recent male visitors. Finding none, she mentally chided herself. Time to focus.

"What about Frank's wife?"

The question stopped Ami short. "What do you mean?"

Gina paused, her sleep-deprived brain finally catching up. "Sorry. You weren't there when Berenstein and I met Tamar. He's Dee's nephew, works at the mini mart next to the gallery. He mentioned Frank's wife in passing, which hit my radar since Frank was definitely giving off single-guy energy at the party."

"No one said anything about a wife." Ami reached for her phone. "I need to tell Detective Talliere."

"One sec." Gina held up a hand. "Let me call Dee first. Maybe she can get us Ms. DeMano's number before we send the cops charging in. Save the boys in blue some time."

"Girls."

"Huh?"

"Girls in blue, actually," Ami said absently. "The lead detective's a woman."

"Right. I knew that." Gina sat down in one of the chairs and scrolled through her contacts while Ami paced, Gertrude weaving between her legs. She tapped out Dee's number and Dee answered quickly.

"Any news?" Dee asked.

"Nothing solid yet, but listen—I need Frank's wife's contact info. The police don't know about her yet."

"Ex-wife, you mean. Whitney. They started the gallery together, divorced three years ago. Though her name's still on the lease." Papers rustled in the background. "Hang on, I keep all the tenant contact info in my maintenance records... had that AC emergency last summer...ah. Got it."

Gina's fingers flew across her phone screen as Dee rattled off the number. "Thanks, Dee. You're saving us a massive amount of time."

After ending the call, Gina immediately started dialing Whitney's number. She noticed Ami's raised eyebrows and shrugged. "Amazing what you can accomplish with a triple-shot latte and three hours of sleep. Now let's see what the ex has to say."

She held her breath, hoping that her phone luck would continue.

One ring. Two rings. Three—

"Whitney Hollister speaking."

Gina blinked in surprise. Hollister, not DeMano. *Interesting.*

"Ms. Hollister? This is Gina Biletti. I'm so sorry to bother you, but I really need to get in touch with Frank for some urgent gallery business." She caught Ami's eye and switched to speaker. "I understand he's in Miami?"

A pause stretched across the line, followed by a dry laugh. "In Miami? Frank told you he was in Miami, did he?"

Ami mouthed *she sounds drunk* and Gina had to agree. It wasn't even nine.

"Uh, yeah. That's what he told his landlord."

"Oh, that's rich. No, he's definitely not here. I'm actually staying at our—well, *my* Miami condo right now." Whitney's voice took on an edge sharp enough to slice paper. "Frank couldn't afford a Miami parking ticket these days, let alone a hotel room. And Art Basel isn't until December, which is the only time he ever has actual business here."

"I see." Gina's fingers drummed against the armrest as a strange pressure built behind her eyes like a headache was coming on. But Gina normally didn't get headaches. Not like this, at least.

Then it hit her—a barrage of images slamming into her brain like photographs being shuffled at lightning speed.

The gallery's dank basement with its moldering boxes.
Old brick tunnel walls snaking into the darkness.
Muddy river water lapping at concrete steps.
A weathered industrial building with high windows reflecting the afternoon sun.

She knew with bone-deep certainty it was a warehouse, though she couldn't explain how she knew, any more than she could explain the metallic taste flooding her mouth or why the room had started to tilt.

Gina closed her eyes until the dizziness passed, then forced her voice steady. "Ms. Hollister, I've been trying to track down inventory records for the gallery. Does Frank have any storage facilities we should check? A warehouse maybe?"

Another pause. "Who are you again, and why are you asking about this?"

Gina's heart thumped against her ribs as she scrambled for a cover story. "Sorry, I'm with Berenstein & Biletti. We're contract adjustors," she said, letting her voice take on a clipped, professional tone. "We're processing an insurance claim for the flooding incident on Thursday. In the gallery basement?"

"Flooding?" Whitney's words slurred slightly. Ice clinked against glass in the background. "Nobody told me about any flooding."

"That's…concerning." Gina spotted Ami's wide-eyed look and held up a finger. "Because I'm seeing both your names as property contacts."

"Typical Frank. Trying to cut me out again. You know what? I'm still on the deed. I should be getting half of any settlement."

"Absolutely. Any claim benefits would need to be properly distributed to all listed parties. I can arrange for separate checks to be issued if you prefer." Gina pressed her advantage. "But first, we need to document everything properly. That includes any auxiliary storage facilities."

A long exhale. "Yeah, there's a place on North Basin Avenue. More of a glorified self-storage unit than anything else. We kept overflow inventory there, old records, that sort of thing." Another clink of ice. "I'll text you the address. But I want a copy of that claim when you're done. Every single item."

"Of course," Gina said, her skin humming with that same electric energy she'd felt in her vision. "You'll have it all in writing."

After Gina ended the call, Ami stared at her in stunned silence. "Where the hell did that come from?"

chapter 17

. . .

Swan Island

GINA AND AMI decided to put a pin in whatever had just happened with that dizzy spell and sudden knowing. They had more pressing matters, but Gina couldn't shake the way Ami kept looking at her like she understood something Gina herself didn't quite grasp yet.

While Ami talked with Detective Talliere on speakerphone about their conversation with Frank's ex-wife, Gina pulled the laptop closer and typed the address from Whitney's text into Google Maps. Gertrude observed her search with regal disdain, tail twitching against the keyboard like some feline metronome marking the passage of precious time.

"Sorry, your highness," Gina murmured, gently scooting her chair over to give the cat more space. "Just need to borrow this corner of the couch for a minute." She wondered if the cat lorded over Morgan's writing sessions like this. Pushing the thought aside, she zoomed in on the industrial area. "Got it! The address is on Swan Island, just north of downtown on the river."

"Excellent," Detective Talliere's crisp voice crackled through the speaker. "We're pushing for an expedited warrant. Already have surveillance teams on the gallery and his condo in Parkrose." A pause filled the room. "No sign of him at either location."

Gina took a final sip from her latte, pushing away the empty cup. The wheels of justice turned way too slowly for her taste. She could practically feel Morgan locked up in that warehouse—assuming she was right. And she *was* right. She knew it the same way she knew her brothers wouldn't call on her birthday or that Viv—

Focus, Gina.

"How long for the warrant?" she asked, not bothering to hide her impatience. Every minute they waited was another minute Morgan spent trapped in whatever nightmare Frank had cooked up for her.

"It depends," Talliere said, her tone measured. "I should have more information by early afternoon."

"What the hell else do you need, Detective?" The words exploded out before Gina could stop them. "Sorry, but…look, we have his ex-wife confirming he lied about Miami. We have a remote location located right on the river—"

"Which we're investigating," Talliere cut in. "I'll call as soon as we have news."

The line went dead, leaving Gina to stare at the laptop screen.

Swan Island's industrial sprawl stretched across the satellite view like a giant concrete jigsaw puzzle. Warehouses, shipping containers, train tracks—the perfect place to hide someone if you didn't want them found. And here they sat in this fancy hotel suite, playing the waiting game while Morgan…

No. Not happening.

Gina picked up her own phone and called Berenstein. "Can you bring the car to the Nines? Like, now? I'll explain when you get here."

Her free hand traced the path from downtown to Swan

Island on the screen. Twenty minutes, maybe less depending on traffic.

"Gina." Ami's voice carried a warning note. "You're not thinking what I think you're thinking…"

"Do you have any binoculars?" Gina got up and started pacing the room, her body humming with nervous energy—or caffeine.

"We can't go there. The police—"

"Apparently need to get their paperwork sorted." The words came out sharp. "And what happens if Frank decides to move her while we're sitting here waiting for a permission slip?"

"And what exactly is our plan if he does?"

"We follow him. We don't let him out of our sight."

Ami collapsed onto the couch next to Gertrude, exhaustion evident in every line of her body. The cat bumped her head against Ami's hand, trying to offer comfort. "Why is he even doing this? It doesn't make sense."

Gina stopped pacing. "Maybe it's a *Misery* thing."

"A what?"

"You know, that old Stephen King movie? Kathy Bates, James Caan…" At Ami's blank look, Gina waved her hand. "Never mind. Point is, Frank's a failed author. Maybe he thinks ghost-writing at gunpoint is his ticket out of obscurity."

"That's…" Ami trailed off, her face going slack. "But that doesn't…I mean, how could he possibly get away with it? Even if he forced her to write his book, the second she was free, she'd tell everyone what happened. The only way his plan would work is if…" Her words stuttered to a stop as the horrible truth sank in.

The silence in the room grew thick enough to choke on. Even Gertrude stopped purring.

"If Morgan never walked away from that warehouse," Gina finished quietly.

FRANK'S WAREHOUSE was only three miles away as the crow flies. They wound through the Pearl District toward their destination, past weathered brick buildings and steel-and-glass towers. Gina gripped the steering wheel tighter as she updated Berenstein.

His eyebrows climbed higher with each detail about Whitney's call and Frank's warehouse. "Brilliant detective work," he said as they merged onto the Fremont Bridge that spanned the river.

"More than just detective work, maybe." Ami's voice floated from the back seat, heavy with meaning.

Gina caught her eye in the rearview mirror. There it was again—that knowing look. But whatever it was would have to wait.

After a brief jog north on I-5, they exited the highway where industrial Portland spread out before them in all its gritty glory. Swan Island was a maze of industrial parks and loading docks. Manufacturing plants and stacks of shipping containers stretched to the horizon, interrupted only by the occasional crane jabbing at the cloudy sky.

The Willamette River gleamed to their right, a constant companion as Gina navigated the quiet streets. Portland's skyline looked impossibly far away now, like they'd crossed into another world entirely.

"There. That's it." Ami pointed to a building. It was sandwiched between a shuttered business center and a roadworks storage lot, crammed with a jumble of forgotten equipment, concrete barriers, chain-link fence panels, and piles of those orange road marker poles.

The warehouse itself was unremarkable—a low-slung rectangle of beige metal siding and mud-brown trim that screamed 1985. A roll-up delivery door dominated the front, flanked by a plain metal entrance door and two high-set windows—perfect for keeping prying eyes out. Or keeping someone in. Gina noted the faded "215" stenciled above the entrance. The numbers had nearly vanished, as if the building itself was trying to disappear.

But the weirdest thing was how familiar it all looked. Like this wasn't the first time she'd been here.

"I'm going to circle around," Gina said. "We can park on the far side. Should give us a view of the entrance." She guided the car past rows of concrete barricades and a heap of sandbags.

Berenstein shifted forward, his seatbelt creaking. "There's a pickup by the door. Frank's, you think?"

"Could be," Gina said. "Looks like something a down-and-out gallery owner might drive."

The faded Ford Ranger sat crooked, like its driver had bigger concerns than proper parking. Or wasn't planning to stay long enough to care. Gina's mind spun out dark possibilities she didn't want to consider.

They settled in to wait, the silence broken only by the infrequent rumble of trucks. After an hour of watching pigeons strut across the construction yard like tiny, feathered security guards, Ami cleared her throat.

"I hate to be that person, but…" She squirmed in her seat. "Those three coffees from this morning are making some urgent demands."

"Huh?" Berenstein glanced back at her from the passenger seat.

"I need the restroom."

"We can't leave now," Gina said, not taking her eyes off the warehouse. "What if—"

"The police will be here soon," Ami cut in, her voice strained. "And I really need to go. Like, now."

"Before we do anything," Berenstein said, "we should at least get that plate number. Give the cops something to run."

"Good point." Gina nodded. "We should—" She broke off as Berenstein looked at her expectantly. "Me?"

"My knee doesn't do well on uneven surfaces." He gestured toward the roadworks yard. "And I'm sure Ami's bladder—"

"Can we not discuss my bladder right now?" Ami squirmed again.

"Fine." Gina unbuckled her seatbelt. "I'll go take a picture of the damn truck." She eased out, careful to close the door quietly. Gravel crunched beneath her feet as she crossed the lot, phone already in hand.

She picked her way around traffic barrels and a massive cable reel, hyperaware of every sound. She was still fifty yards from the truck when the warehouse door opened with a metallic groan. Her stomach dropped. *Crap!*

She spun in place, scanning for cover.

An old backhoe sat abandoned near a pile of concrete forms, its orange paint dulled to rust. She dove behind its massive tire, pressing herself against the hard rubber.

Frank emerged wearing dad jeans and a denim jacket, his head swiveling like a paranoid owl before pulling the door shut. Even from here, she could read the tension in his movements as he hurried to his truck.

Gina hardly dared to breathe. The truck's door slammed shut, and the engine coughed to life.

She waited until the pickup disappeared around the corner. No sudden brake lights, no suggestion that he'd spotted Berenstein and Ami.

Her legs felt like overcooked pasta as she approached the entrance. The door would be locked, of course, but she reached for the handle anyway.

It turned with a low squeal of protest, and the door swung open.

chapter 18

. . .

Like Herpes?

THE SMELL of damp wood and musty paper enveloped Gina as she stepped inside the dim space. She hesitated in the hallway, every true crime podcast she'd ever listened to screaming at her to turn back. But the same instinct that had led her here—that weird certainty she couldn't explain—pushed her forward.

Shadows stretched across a maze of storage rooms branching off a central corridor. Wooden crates loomed like misshapen sentries. Metal shelves sagged under yellowing document boxes. Even a few forlorn pieces of art leaned against the walls, their frames collecting dust like abandoned hopes.

And there, threading through it all—music. The soft strains of Brandi Carlile's voice floated from somewhere deeper in the building. *Harder to Forgive.* Not exactly the soundtrack she'd expected for a kidnapping.

Gina's footsteps echoed softly as she followed the faint music. The sound led her through a warren of storage spaces until she reached a door that glowed around its edges with warm light.

She held her breath as she eased the door open, fingers trembling against the metal handle.

The sight stopped her cold. A woman sat hunched over a laptop, fingers flying across the keys like she was racing against some invisible deadline. It took Gina several confused heartbeats to recognize her as Morgan Mallory, and even then her brain struggled to reconcile this version with the witchy goddess who had been snatched from the gallery.

Gone were the dramatic red wig and gothic wardrobe—instead, Morgan wore faded yoga pants and an oversized sweater, her natural brown hair cut in a practical bob. Without the signature winged eyeliner and jangling crystal jewelry, she looked startlingly ordinary—except for that star tattoo still glinting at the corner of her eye, the last remnant of her magical persona.

The space around her was a bizarre mix of office and dorm room—narrow bed shoved against one wall, sad little kitchenette in the corner, even a couple of beanbag chairs that looked like they'd been rescued from some 1970s garage sale.

Morgan spun at the sound of the door, her face registering genuine shock. "Gina? What are you—how did you find—" She broke off, something unreadable flickering across her expression that made the hair on the back of Gina's neck stand up.

"Are you okay?" Gina scanned for signs of restraints or injuries. Her eyes caught on the laptop screen—definitely words, definitely a manuscript. Oh god. Her *Misery* theory wasn't just paranoia.

"What are you doing here?" Morgan's brow furrowed.

"Rescuing you, obviously."

Morgan just sat there, seemingly lost in thought.

"We need to go," Gina said. "Frank just left, but who knows when he'll be back."

"Where's Ami?"

"In the car with Berenstein. Come on—"

"I can't." Morgan gestured at the laptop. "I have to finish this. For Frank."

A chill crept up Gina's spine. *Classic Stockholm Syndrome.* She'd read about this. "Listen to me. Whatever Frank's done to make you think you have to do this—"

"No, you don't understand." Morgan pushed back from the desk, rubbing her temples. "I *want* to be here."

The words hit Gina like a slap. She stared at Morgan, at the comfortable setup, at the distinct lack of chains or hand-cuffs or any signs of duress. And the unlocked door. The reality of the situation started to seep in.

"What exactly am I not understanding?" Gina asked, suddenly feeling like she'd walked into the wrong story entirely.

"Frank is helping me." Morgan's voice held a note of desperation, like she was trying to convince herself as much as Gina. "He understands what I'm trying to—"

The door crashed open behind them. Ami burst in with Berenstein huffing behind her, both of them skidding to a stop at the sight of Morgan sitting calmly at her desk. Ami's face cycled through shock, relief, and then shock again.

"Leigh!" Ami flew across the room and threw her arms around her friend's shoulders. "Did he hurt you? We thought—"

The distant, insistent wail of sirens pierced the warehouse. Morgan's face drained of color, her facade of calm crumbling.

"I am so screwed."

THE COLUMBIA RIVER stretched beside them, steel-grey under a cloudy sky. Gina steered around another curve, barely noticing the gorgeous views as they headed home to Maiden-well. Her mind was too full of yesterday's revelations to care about the scenery.

"I still can't believe it," Berenstein said, breaking their twenty-minute silence. He'd been unusually quiet since they'd left Portland. "I mean, faking your own kidnapping to escape fame? That's some next-level drama."

"This from a man who got knee injections just to attend a book signing." Gina kept her eyes on the road, wondering if she'd ever see Morgan—Leigh—again.

The whole scene at the warehouse kept replaying in her mind on an endless loop. The cops swarming in, Detective Talliere's stern face softening to disbelief as Leigh explained her elaborate exit strategy. How she'd enlisted Frank to help stage her "kidnapping" in exchange for ghostwriting his novel. All so she could disappear into a normal life with Emerson, leaving her famous witchy persona behind.

"Poor Ami," Berenstein sighed. "Finding out your best friend trusted you so little she'd rather let you think she'd been kidnapped…"

"Because she couldn't risk the Trainers finding out." Gina caught his questioning look. "Her publisher, too. Apparently, they're not the type to let their golden goose fly away quietly."

The rest of the drive passed in comfortable silence, but Gina's mind kept circling back to her final conversation with Leigh.

They'd found a moment alone while the police were taking statements, tucked into a corner of the warehouse.

"I'm so sorry for dragging you into this," Leigh had said. "Though I have to admit, you showing up here was never part of the plan."

The admission hit Gina like a splash of cold water. "Really? What about that weird prophecy? Ami told me that you said I'd be the one to find you."

"That wasn't a prophecy." Something tight and anxious crept into Leigh's voice. "It was a warning. I was trying to tell her to keep you away, no matter what happened. I planned to warn you directly at the party, but then…" Her hand fluttered vaguely in the air. "Well, that woman tried to spike my drink, and…"

Gina's mouth went desert-dry. "Wait a second, you *didn't* want me to find you?"

"It would have been better for everyone if you hadn't."

"Better?" The word shot out, as sharp as broken glass. She thought about Ami's sleepless nights, the fear in her eyes. "What you did to Ami was cruel. She cares about you so much."

"I know." Leigh hugged herself like she was trying to hold something in. "Not telling her was my second bad decision. I'll work to make that right."

"Good luck with that." Gina turned to go, her boots scraping against the concrete floor, but Leigh's next words froze her mid-step.

"There's something else. That thing you felt when we first met at the reading—that was real."

The memory of that electric jolt hit Gina all over again, that moment of impossible knowing that she'd been trying to file away under 'weird shit to never think about again.' Her chest squeezed tight. "What are you talking about?"

"You have the Gift," Leigh said, her voice barely above a whisper. "I gave it to you. Just like another woman gave it to me… years ago."

"I don't understand."

"Neither do I, not really." Leigh's voice had dropped to barely above a whisper. "It's something mysterious that gets passed between people."

"Like herpes?" The joke had slipped out before Gina could stop it.

Leigh had laughed then, a genuine sound that seemed to brighten the dingy warehouse. "Hopefully much better than that. I hope you put it to good use."

Now, as the river rolled beside them carrying its own

mysteries toward the sea, Gina wondered what exactly she was supposed to do with this Gift—assuming it was real and not just another piece of Morgan Mallory's elaborate fiction.

The gorge's towering cliffs threw long shadows across the highway. Somewhere ahead, Maidenwell waited with its own secrets. But for now, Gina was content to let the miles unspool beneath her wheels, carrying her away from one mystery and toward whatever waited next.

the gift

A Bonus Novella

one

. . .

Responsible Finances

FIVE YEARS AGO…

```
Miranda's footsteps echoed through the
empty hospital corridor.
```

LEIGH DOLAN DELETED the sentence for the fourth time in twenty minutes, her cursor blinking accusingly in the Microsoft Word document hidden behind her quarterly marketing presentation. The conference room's fluorescent lights cast a sickly glow over her laptop screen, making the blank page seem even more sterile than usual.

"—and as you can see from these heat maps, user engagement peaked during our Medicare supplement awareness campaign—" Brad from Digital Optimization (whose last name Leigh had never bothered to learn) droned on, his voice a perfect match for the room's humming lights.

Leigh typed the sentence again:

```
Miranda's footsteps echoed through the
empty hospital corridor.
```

She'd written and deleted those words forty-seven times since starting her latest novel six months ago. The number matched her collection of rejection letters with a symmetry that felt almost purposeful.

"Leigh?" Sharon Whitman's voice cut through her thoughts. "Do you have those Medicare Advantage numbers ready?"

"Sure do." Leigh smoothly alt-tabbed to her PowerPoint presentation, muscle memory taking over. Her desktop background—a stock photo of a Zen garden she'd chosen during a brief meditation phase—flashed between windows. "Our Q1 metrics show a 12% increase in online lead generation compared to last year's numbers."

The graphs and charts flowed past with practiced precision. Leigh could have given this presentation in her sleep (and sometimes did, according to her ex-husband Noah, back when she still had someone to monitor her sleep-talking). Her voice maintained its perfect professional cadence while her mind wandered back to Miranda, alone in that hospital corridor, waiting for something to happen.

"Excellent work as always, Leigh." Sharon's smile reminded Leigh of her mother's real estate headshot—warm but calculated. "Which is why I'd like you to take point on our new Instagram initiative. We need to establish a stronger social media presence, really connect with a younger demographic."

Leigh's pencil skirt suddenly felt too tight, like a snake slowly constricting around her thighs. "Absolutely. I'd be happy to research some strategies," she said, already mentally rearranging her weekend writing schedule. The novel would have to wait. Again.

"Perfect." Sharon tapped her Mont Blanc pen against her leather portfolio. "We'll need a preliminary content calendar by next Friday. Brad can share his engagement metrics to help inform the strategy."

Brad perked up at the mention of his metrics, but Leigh was already gone, mentally composing Instagram captions about the exciting world of term life insurance. #blessed #adulting #responsiblefinances

The meeting dragged on for another forty-five minutes. Leigh's notebook filled with bullet points about social media best practices, while in the margins, Miranda waited in her hospital corridor, frozen between footsteps, going nowhere.

AN HOUR LATER, Leigh opened her laptop in a corner of the break room, balancing her sad sandwich beside it. The Medicare Part D campaign document lurked in one window, while her novel draft glowed accusingly in another. Her fingers hovered over the keys as she tried to make Miranda's footsteps echo convincingly down that hospital corridor. The words refused to come.

The microwave hummed. Someone's leftover fish from two days ago created an invisible force field of smell around the kitchen area. The Keurig sputtered and dripped, marking time like a broken metronome. Leigh barely noticed any of it, lost in her attempts to make the scene work.

"I'm pretty sure those aren't the campaign metrics Sharon was asking about." Dawn's voice snapped Leigh back to reality. Her friend leaned in over her shoulder, wearing the knowing smile of someone who'd caught her teenage daughter texting instead of doing homework. "Unless Miranda's taking that lonely walk down the hospital corridor to sign up for prescription drug coverage?" She raised an eyebrow. "Though that could actually work as a marketing angle…"

Leigh quickly minimized the document. "Just multitasking." She spun her chair to face Dawn, whose long sweater (the color of approaching thunderclouds) matched her knowing expression. "Did you need the Q1 numbers for the sales team?"

"What I need is for my friend to stop hiding behind Medicare statistics." Dawn perched on the edge of the lunch table, her presence blocking the worst of the fluorescent glare. "Have you thought any more about sending your book to Mila?"

The mention of Dawn's sister—a real-life literary agent in New York with real-life connections to real-life publishers—sent a familiar spike of anxiety through Leigh's chest. "I'm still polishing the manuscript," she lied, the same excuse she'd been using for months.

"You can't keep your novel hidden on your hard drive forever," Dawn said.

"Watch me." Leigh turned back to her computer, pulling up a spreadsheet of keyword analytics. "Speaking of things that can't wait forever, Sharon wants a full Instagram strategy by next Friday."

"Instagram?" Dawn's eyebrows rose. "For insurance?"

"Apparently we need to connect with the youths." Leigh affected her best Sharon Whitman voice. "Nothing says 'living your best life' like a properly structured whole life policy."

Dawn laughed, but her eyes remained concerned. "Just promise me you won't let the corporate content completely take over. Your writing deserves—"

"I should really get started on this strategy." Leigh gestured at her screen, where Google displayed "How to make insurance interesting on social media" with zero promising results. "Sharon's expecting—"

"I know, I know." Dawn stood, adjusting her cardigan. "But think about Mila, okay? Sometimes the scariest steps are the most important ones."

After Dawn left, Leigh opened a new Excel spreadsheet. Column A: Instagram Strategy. Column B: Novel Revisions.

The cells stared back at her, empty and accusatory. She found herself doing the math: eight hours at work, minus getting ready for work, minus commuting, minus meetings, minus lunch break, minus interruptions… carry the one… divide by anxiety… equals approximately forty-five minutes of actual creative writing time per day.

Her phone buzzed against the break room table. A calendar notification lit up the screen: "Charlie—2:30." Between her color-coded work calendar and meticulously maintained submission spreadsheet, this was the only reminder that appeared with irregular frequency, popping up seven or eight times a year like a morse code of responsibility.

She glanced at her Instagram strategy document (current word count: zero). Her elderly neighbor's appointment had slipped her mind completely, buried under marketing metrics and stalled creativity. The medical building was twenty minutes away in Hartford's mid-afternoon traffic, which meant she'd need to head back to their apartment building by 2:00.

Charlie would be waiting in his doorway four units down from hers, just like always. In the thirteen months since she'd first offered him a ride, she'd learned his patterns: the careful checking of his wallet, the way he'd pat his coat pockets three times before leaving, how he'd grip the doorframe slightly when turning to lock up. She'd never asked what the appointments were for. The way he looked afterward told her enough.

"You must be busy with important business things," he'd say, like he did every time, shifting his slight frame against the doorway. The top of his head barely reached Leigh's shoulder, even when she wore flats. "I can find another way."

"The insurance industry will survive without me for two hours." She'd shoulder his worn leather messenger bag, pretending not to notice how he leaned against the wall. "Besides, who else would tell me train stories on the drive?"

His stories had become as much a part of their routine as his triple-check of his pockets or her careful attention to potholes. The April sun slanted through her car windows as Charlie settled into the passenger seat, his wool coat still buttoned despite the spring warmth.

"You know what this weather reminds me of?" His voice carried the particular warmth of someone about to share a favorite memory. "Back when I was conducting the New Haven line, spring days like this were the best. Sun hitting the water just right." He gestured vaguely eastward. "Had this one passenger—must have been in her seventies—who took the 6:15 every Friday to visit her sister in Boston. Always wore these elegant wool suits, even in summer."

Leigh's writer brain filed away the detail about the wool suits, the kind of specific observation that made characters feel real on the page. "Did she do that year-round?"

"Rain or shine, January to December. Called me Carlton for ten years straight." He chuckled, then winced slightly as they hit a bump. "Started saving her favorite seat—third row from the front, water side. Had a perfect view of the Sound all the way up the coast. Never told her, just made sure it was free. Little things matter when you're making the same journey over and over."

The medical building's parking lot sprawled ahead, identical to a dozen others scattered across Hartford's suburbs. Charlie's tight grip on the door handle told her this wasn't the time to ask follow-up questions about the wool-suited passenger. Some stories were better left for the drive home, when he'd be too drained to talk anyway.

She found a spot close to the entrance, knowing he'd insist on walking in unassisted but wanting to minimize the distance. The routine was well-established: she'd wait in the lobby with her laptop while he disappeared behind one of the many unmarked doors. They never discussed which doctor he saw or why. Some mysteries, like some stories, didn't need explaining.

Her laptop whirred to life, the cursor still blinking accusingly at Miranda's unfinished footsteps. But now those hospital corridors felt different, colored by thoughts of Charlie's train stories and wool-suited passengers making their weekly pilgrimages. Maybe Miranda needed her own rituals, her own careful checking of pockets and counting of steps. Maybe the echo of her footsteps carried more than just plot momentum.

The waiting room's institutional beige walls managed to be both bland and somehow aggressive in their blandness. Leigh shifted in the molded plastic chair, trying to find a position that wouldn't leave her back screaming. She'd written three versions of Miranda's footsteps in the past hour, each one echoing more hollowly than the last.

A girl who couldn't be more than sixteen sat across from her, tearing a magazine subscription card into increasingly tiny pieces. Her heavy eyeliner, leather jacket (trying too hard to look worn), and carefully ripped jeans (definitely purchased that way) screamed suburban rebellion. Each time the door opened, the girl's head snapped up with the kind of desperation Leigh recognized from too many similar rooms, too many similar waits.

The teenager's anxiety radiated across the space between them, her leg bouncing with barely contained energy as she reduced another subscription card to confetti. The motion reminded Leigh of Charlie's triple-check of his pockets, those small rituals people created when control felt just out of reach. Her own ritual involved these waiting room writing sessions, though Miranda's footsteps still refused to carry her anywhere meaningful.

The girl's hands shook slightly as she reached for yet another magazine. Something in her determined effort to appear unfazed touched a familiar chord in Leigh. She'd written enough characters trapped in moments of uncertain waiting to recognize the weight of it—that peculiar suspended animation where time stretched like taffy and every opening door carried both hope and dread.

Leigh caught the girl's eye and smiled, trying to convey what she'd learned from these institutional beige rooms and their uncomfortable chairs: that waiting ended, one way or another, and strength often came from unexpected places. The girl's tight shoulders relaxed slightly, a ghost of a grateful smile touching her lips.

When the door opened again, a woman in a purple cardigan emerged. The girl was up and moving before Leigh could process the motion, magazine fragments scattering like autumn leaves.

"Mom?"

"All clear, baby. Just like I said."

Leigh turned back to her laptop, giving mother and daughter privacy for their relief. In her mind, Miranda's footsteps took on a new rhythm, echoing with the particular resonance of waiting room survivors everywhere.

An hour later, the door opened for Charlie. He emerged pale and slightly unsteady, but his expression carried the particular determination of someone who declined to be pushed in a wheelchair. Leigh packed up her laptop with practiced efficiency, taking his bag before he could protest.

The afternoon sun had shifted, painting the parking lot in long shadows. Charlie's hand trembled slightly on her arm as she guided him to the car, but his dignity remained intact. The drive home started in comfortable silence, broken only by the soft hum of the heater.

"You know what I miss most?" Charlie's voice was rougher than usual, barely above a whisper.

"What's that?" Leigh asked.

"The sound of the tracks at night. They'd sing, especially after rain. Each section had its own voice." His eyes were closed, but his hand moved slightly, conducting an invisible symphony. "Modern trains, they're all wrong. Too smooth. But back then… you could read the whole line by its song."

At the next stoplight, Leigh pulled out her phone, fingers trembling slightly as she typed "tracks singing after rain" into her notes. The phrase felt like a something special, delicate and rare—something she needed to preserve even if she didn't yet understand why.

In the passenger seat, Charlie's face relaxed in sleep, years falling away from his features. Whatever dreams visited him now, Leigh hoped they carried the music of those rain-washed tracks, their song echoing across the decades like a message in a bottle, waiting for someone to hear it.

two

. . .

#StillHaveMyDayJob

BACK AT WORK, the afternoon dissolved into a blur of browser tabs: social media marketing blogs, competitor Instagram accounts, and occasionally, when she thought no one was looking, literary agent submission guidelines. She organized them meticulously in separate Chrome windows, each one labeled and arranged by priority—a habit she'd developed in her first week at Roxawan Insurance and never abandoned. Every time she switched back to her novel, Miranda stood frozen in that hospital corridor, waiting for something to happen. Just like her creator.

The office emptied gradually as her coworkers drifted away, their conversations about weekend plans and new restaurants fading into silence. Leigh stayed anchored to her desk, making up the time she'd spent driving Charlie. Her dedication to Roxawan had become almost reflexive after four years—she'd never been the type to leave tasks unfinished, even when they involved crafting social media strategies about term life insurance.

Leigh's mother had always praised her dependability, though sometimes the word felt more like a life sentence than a compliment. Her desk lamp cast a small circle of light in the growing darkness, like a spotlight on an empty stage. By seven-fifteen, the building had grown quiet enough to hear the heating system cycling down, the familiar sounds of corporate architecture settling into its evening routine.

The drive to her apartment in Hartford's West End felt quicker at this hour, probably because she'd memorized the exact timing of every traffic light between the office and home. Leigh spent it mentally composing Instagram captions, each one more desperate than the last.

Living your best life starts with planning for your death! #InsuranceGoals #AdultingHard.

She'd never quite understood the appeal of social media—her own Instagram account had exactly three posts, all from years ago when she'd briefly attempted to "build her author platform" according to the Creative Penn Podcast's advice.

Two years ago, she would have been driving home to the house in West Hartford instead—the beautiful colonial with the wrap-around porch that she and Noah had restored together. She missed that house viscerally, far more than she missed her ex-husband. The practical part of her brain had already calculated exactly how many years of saving it would take to afford a similar home on her own (twelve, assuming no major market changes and an aggressive investment strategy). Sometimes she still caught herself taking the exit to their old neighborhood out of habit, muscle memory refusing to accept the downgrade to her current living situation.

Her cramped one-bedroom greeted her with its familiar mix of fast furniture and aspirational writer decor, everything arranged with the precise organization that helped her maintain sanity in limited square footage. A vintage typewriter she'd never used (purchased during what Noah used to call her "Hemingway phase") competed for precious surface area with her coffee maker. Her wall of color-coded bookshelves—organized first by genre, then alphabetically, with a separate Excel sheet tracking loans to friends—made the room feel even smaller.

Virginia Woolf stared down from her framed poster with an expression that seemed to judge Leigh's reduced circumstances and practical wardrobe choices. The whole place smelled faintly of the lavender candle she'd lit that morning and forgotten to blow out—now just a sad puddle of wax in a jar, a rare lapse in her usually meticulous attention to fire safety.

Leigh kicked off her sensible heels (the ones she'd bought specifically for presentations, with their optimistic "all-day comfort" promise and their complete indifference to current trends) and opened her laptop one last time. Her shoes joined the neat row by the door, arranged by frequency of use rather than style—a system that would have horrified her more fashionable coworkers. The email she'd been avoiding all day sat unopened in her inbox, its sender's name—Palgrave-Mills Literary Agency—making her stomach clench.

She poured a glass of wine before taking a deep breath and finally opening the email.

The rejection was professionally crafted, almost kind in its dismissal:

Dear Ms. Dolan,
Thank you for submitting "The Girl in Suite 23." While your strong voice and technical skill impressed us, we regret to inform you that this project is not quite right for our list…

Leigh added the response to her tracking spreadsheet, a document so meticulously maintained it would have impressed her company's auditors. Row 48 filled out with familiar categories: Date Sent, Agency, Agent Name, Response Time, Form Rejection (Y/N), Personal Notes. She'd even created pivot tables to analyze rejection patterns by month and agent response types. The data stretched back eighteen months, a perfect record of failure rendered in Microsoft Excel.

She stared at the screen, at the neat rows cataloging her literary ambitions. Six manuscripts. Two of them self-published under a pen name after the rejection pile grew too depressing—romantic suspense novels that had earned her exactly twenty-six sales and one review (two stars, complaining about formatting issues, which still stung because she'd triple-checked the formatting). The other four had been submitted everywhere, polite rejections accumulating like parking tickets. Each "thanks but no thanks" email felt like confirmation of what she'd always suspected: that she was exactly what her mother had accused her of being—a marketing manager playing at being a writer.

She opened her novel document again, determined to push past that single sentence, just as she'd pushed through every other obstacle in her life with methodical persistence. The cursor blinked between "hospital" and "corridor," like a metronome counting beats of silence. The wine glass sat untouched beside her keyboard, precisely positioned on a coaster to protect the IKEA desk she'd assembled with mathematical precision.

```
Miranda's footsteps echoed through the
empty hospital corridor.
```

Delete.

```
Miranda's footsteps echoed—
```

Delete.

```
Miranda—
```

Delete.

Her fingers moved with the same efficiency she applied to quarterly reports, each keystroke precise and purposeful even in failure. Outside her window, Hartford's nighttime skyline glittered with promise, each light representing someone else's story. Leigh wondered how many other would-be novelists sat at their computers right now, deleting and rewriting the same sentences, trapped between the lives they had and the lives they wanted.

Her phone buzzed with a calendar reminder: "Instagram Strategy Meeting—9 a.m."

The corporate world marched on, indifferent to her creative struggles, but at least it offered the comfort of clear metrics and achievable goals.

She had exactly fourteen hours to figure out how to make term life insurance appeal to millennials, a task she'd already broken down into subsections in her planning document.

Leigh closed her laptop without saving the document, though she'd already backed it up to three different cloud services. Miranda could wait another day in her hospital corridor. After all, she'd been waiting there for three months already—what was one more night of silence?

In the dark reflection of her window, Leigh caught a glimpse of herself: smartphone in one hand, wine glass in the other, Virginia Woolf judging her life choices from the wall behind her. The scene could have been a perfect Instagram post:

Living that #WriterLife! #AmWriting #StillHaveMyDayJob

But she didn't take the picture. Instead, she turned away from the window and reached for the TV remote. There was probably a Lifetime movie on somewhere, something to fill the silence until tomorrow, when she'd put her sensible heels back on and return to her sensible job with its sensible disappointments.

The wine remained untouched, a ruby reminder of another evening spent not writing. In the morning, she'd pour it down the drain and pretend she'd never opened the bottle. Just like she'd pretend she'd never opened that rejection email, never written that sentence about Miranda, never dreamed of being anything more than a marketing manager who was really good at tracking metrics.

Some dreams were better left in spreadsheets, safely contained in cells where they couldn't hurt anyone. At least spreadsheets followed rules you could understand.

three

· · ·

Speaking of Growth Opportunities...

THE THURSDAY NIGHT crowd at the Half Door Irish Pub fell firmly into two categories: young professionals pretending their jobs didn't exhaust them, and older regulars who had long ago stopped pretending. Leigh and Ami's usual corner table existed somewhere between these worlds, much like their relationship existed somewhere between friendship and family.

"So how bad was it?" Ami set down her Aperol Spritz on the scratched wooden table. Her glasses caught the neon beer signs' glow, briefly giving her an otherworldly appearance.

"The usual form letter." Leigh took a long sip of her drink, letting the vodka tonic burn away the day's mediocrity. "Strong voice, technical skill, not quite right for their list. At least they spelled my name correctly this time. And Dawn won't stop pushing me to send it to her sister—you know, the literary agent? She cornered me in the break room again today."

"Rejection letter number what?"

"Forty-seven. No, forty-eight." Leigh traced a water ring on the table. "I have a spreadsheet."

"Of course you do." Ami's smile carried the same fond

exasperation she probably used with her third graders. "Only you would turn literary rejection into a data analysis project. But maybe Dawn's right about—"

The rest of her sentence disappeared as a man in a rumpled Brooks Brothers suit swayed past their table for the third time, his attention fixed on Ami. His wedding ring caught the bar's dim light—a detail Leigh noted with the same instinct that made her track conversion metrics.

"Speaking of analysis," Ami said, shifting closer to Leigh as the man lingered nearby, "I saw Noah at Mom and Dad's on Sunday. He brought Ellie."

The cocktail turned bitter on Leigh's tongue. "How was that?"

"Awkward. Mom kept calling her Emily." Ami's hand found Leigh's on the table, a practiced move as the Brooks Brothers suit drew nearer. "But not as awkward as this is about to be," she murmured to Leigh, then raised her voice slightly. "Honey, remember when we first met?"

Leigh squeezed her hand, falling into their familiar choreography. She could probably recite this script in her sleep by now, their little production honed over countless Thursday nights. "How could I forget? You were wearing that ridiculous paint-covered smock."

"It was fashion!" Ami protested, her voice carrying just enough to reach their hovering observer. She leaned in closer, her long dark curls brushing Leigh's shoulder. "And you still fell in love with me."

The suit retreated, probably to report back to his equally married friends at the bar. Leigh kept hold of Ami's hand, their fingers intertwined in a comfortable lie. They'd perfected this routine over four years of friendship, building an elaborate fictional romance complete with first date details and anniversary traditions. It was easier than explaining the real story: that Ami was her ex-husband's sister, that their friendship had survived her divorce and Ami's assault, that sometimes the family you choose matters more than the family you marry into.

"Ellie's teaching Noah to cook," Ami said once the suit was safely out of earshot. "He made paella."

"Noah once burned microwave popcorn so badly we had to paint the kitchen ceiling." The memory didn't hurt as much as it used to. "Good for him, though. Personal growth and all that."

"Speaking of growth opportunities—" Ami's grin turned wicked. "Tell me more about this Instagram strategy you mentioned in your texts. Please tell me Roxawan Insurance is finally entering the twenty-first century."

Leigh groaned. "Sharon wants us to 'connect with the youths.' Her words, not mine. How do I make term life insurance appeal to millennials?"

"Easy." Ami pulled out her phone. "Just add some skull emojis and call it #DeathGoals."

The laughter bubbled up before Leigh could stop it, genuine and freeing. This was why Thursday nights at the Half Door mattered—not just the cocktails, or the fake-dating strategy, but these moments when the absurdity of life became something they could share rather than endure.

"You're not actually going to suggest skull emojis to Sharon, are you?" Ami's eyes widened with mock horror. "Because I need you to record that meeting if you do."

"I was thinking more along the lines of aspirational lifestyle posts." Leigh pulled up Roxawan's sad excuse for an Instagram feed on her phone. "You know, young professionals drinking oat milk lattes while signing their first life insurance policies. #Adulting."

"Your soul just died a little saying that, didn't it?"

"My soul's been dead since they made me write a blog post called '10 Reasons Medicare Part D Is Totally Lit.'"

A fresh round of drinks appeared, courtesy of a bartender who'd served them long enough to know their Thursday pattern. Leigh noticed Ami's glass was still half full—unusual for someone who normally matched her drink for drink.

"Everything okay?" Leigh nodded toward the Aperol Spritz. "You're falling behind."

"Parent-teacher conferences tomorrow." Ami pushed her glasses up with one paint-stained finger. "I need to be clear-headed to explain to Mrs. Gunderson why her precious Dakota's artistic vision shouldn't involve eating the paste."

"Dakota?"

"Twin sister to McKenzie. Not to be confused with McKinley in my other class."

The Brooks Brothers suit made another pass, this time with reinforcements—a slightly less rumpled friend whose tie suggested an afternoon of client meetings followed by liquid dinner.

Ami didn't miss a beat. "Remember our first Valentine's Day? When you tried to recreate our first date but the restaurant had closed down?"

"We ended up eating gas station sushi in your car." Leigh leaned in, their prepared script feeling oddly comfortable. "Still the most romantic food poisoning I've ever had."

Their lips met in a soft kiss that lasted just long enough to be convincing. As the suits retreated, Leigh found herself thinking that she'd now kissed Noah's sister more times than she'd ever kissed Noah himself. The thought should have been uncomfortable, but instead it felt like some strange piece of personal trivia, filed away with all her other collected oddities.

Ami's thumb traced absent patterns on Leigh's palm, a gesture that felt both familiar and strange. They'd played this game so many times over the years that sometimes the lines between performance and reality blurred, like one of Ami's paintings left out in the rain.

Her friend pulled back slightly, her expression shifting to something more serious. "You know we can't keep doing this forever," she said softly. "One of these days we're going to have to get real boyfriends."

Leigh rested her head against Ami's shoulder, breathing in the familiar scent of poster paint and Elmer's glue that always clung to her friend's clothes. "Never," she declared, but her playful tone couldn't quite mask the protective surge she felt. For Ami to even mention dating was surprising progress—like seeing the first spring bulb pushing through winter soil.

The memory surfaced unbidden: Ami's roommate calling at 3 a.m., Leigh still half-asleep as she drove to the hospital, the fluorescent lights making everything feel surreal. Eighteen months hadn't dulled the horror of that night.

Ami's new boyfriend, Michael, had seemed so normal— right up until he slipped a roofie into Ami's drink. If her roommate hadn't come home early…

Leigh suppressed a shiver, her hand tightening instinctively around Ami's. The aftermath had been brutal. Even though the drugs had mercifully erased most of Ami's memories of that night, the trauma had carved deep channels through her life. For months, she'd barely left her apartment except to teach. Her vibrant paintings had turned dark, apocalyptic. She'd stopped meeting friends for dinner, stopped dating, stopped trusting.

But now here she was, starting to make jokes about boyfriends again. It wasn't much, but it felt like a small miracle, like watching something precious and fragile slowly knitting itself back together.

The moment shattered as Leigh's phone buzzed against the table, the screen lighting up with Sharon's name. Her boss had the kind of boundary issues that made sovereign nations nervous.

"Don't pretend you didn't see that," Ami said as Leigh tried to slide the phone face-down. "She'll just keep calling."

The message glowed accusingly:

> Need you to call me back ASAP re: the
> Bridgeport campaign.

ASAP in Sharon-speak meant 'drop whatever meaningless personal activity you're engaged in and attend to my whims.'

"Take it. Go save the world of insurance marketing." Ami waved her off. "I'll draw."

The bass from the Half Door's ancient sound system was reaching seismic levels, so Leigh grabbed her coat and bag and headed for the door, grateful at least that the spring air would help clear her head. Behind her, she could hear someone requesting "Sweet Caroline" for what had to be the fourth time that night.

She stepped outside, fishing in her bag for the pack of American Spirits she'd promised herself she'd never touch again when she turned thirty. *Four months left to break that promise,* she thought, lighting up with practiced guilt. The nicotine hit her system as Sharon's name pulsed on her screen, both familiar vices that she really should have outgrown by now.

Through the Half Door's window, she watched Ami pull out her sketchbook—the one she always carried for moments of inspiration. In the neon-tinted glass, their reflection fractured into multiple possible stories: two women in a bar, playing at romance, hiding from real connection behind a comfortable script. The cigarette smoke curled between Leigh and her reflection, adding another layer of distance, another barrier between who she was and who she'd planned to be at thirty.

Leigh tapped Sharon's number, bracing herself for whatever marketing emergency had manifested over dinner. Her boss answered on the first ring.

"I'm so sorry to bother you after hours," Sharon said, sounding genuinely apologetic. The woman saved her humanity for true crises, which meant this was going to be bad.

"It's fine. What's up?" Leigh took a long drag of her cigarette, watching a couple stumble out of the bar.

"I just got back from dinner with the Bridgeport DataSys team." Sharon paused, and Leigh could practically see her pinching the bridge of her nose. "They want to go in a completely new direction with the campaign."

Of course they did. The Bridgeport team treated marketing strategies like dating apps—always convinced something better might come along if they just kept swiping. Leigh had three different versions of their campaign stored on her laptop, each one abandoned mid-development.

"They had some interesting ideas over drinks," Sharon continued, her tone suggesting 'interesting' was doing a lot of heavy lifting. "I need you to come in early tomorrow—seven a.m. Emergency planning meeting. I'll walk you through it."

Sharon rushed on before Leigh could respond. "I know it's awful timing, but my calendar is completely packed tomorrow. This is literally the only window."

"No problem," Leigh said. "I'll be there." The neon beer signs in the Half Door's window cast her reflection in alternating red and blue, like a warning light.

"Thank you, Leigh." Sharon's relief was palpable. "I know I always come to you with these last-minute things, and I really appreciate how you always manage to make it work."

The praise settled uncomfortably in Leigh's stomach, mixing with her three vodka tonics and the overcooked sliders. Being reliable was supposed to feel better than this, wasn't it? Instead, it felt like another role she'd perfected: Leigh Dolan, dependable marketing manager, who never said no to late-night calls or early-morning meetings.

Back inside the Half Door, the warmth hit her like a wall, carrying the familiar mix of stale beer and faded ambitions. Ami looked up from her sketchbook, her charcoal-smudged fingers wrapped around her still-full Aperol Spritz. "Everything okay in insurance land?"

"Seven a.m. meeting tomorrow." Leigh sat back in her chair, the legs squeaking against the floor. "Sharon's in crisis mode. Again. There goes my pre-work writing session."

"You mean your pre-work staring-at-the-cursor session?" Ami closed her sketchbook, but not before Leigh caught a glimpse of what looked like a self-portrait. "You have so much talent, so much creativity, and you're letting that soul-sucking job drain it all away."

"What am I supposed to do, quit?" Leigh's fingers drummed against her empty glass. "I've got six figures in student loans. Maybe the loan people will accept short stories instead of payments while I pursue my dreams of becoming an artiste."

"No, it doesn't have to be so dramatic. You can compartmentalize—that's what I do. Leave Insurance Drone Leigh at the office. When you come home, you're Author Leigh."

Before Leigh could tell Ami that she'd tried compartmentalizing, a new voice cut through their conversation. "Can I buy you ladies a drink?" A man in a pink button-down hovered by their table, his confidence probably boosted by whatever was in his glass.

Without missing a beat, Ami reached across the table and took Leigh's hand. "Sorry, we're celebrating our anniversary. Three wonderful years." She lifted their joined hands, tenderly kissing Leigh's knuckles.

"Four years," Leigh corrected, falling into their routine. "Remember? We count from the paint store incident."

Pink Shirt retreated, but Ami didn't release Leigh's hand immediately. "Promise me something?"

"If it's about compartmentalizing—"

"Talk to that agent. Dawn's sister?" Ami squeezed her hand once before letting go. "Send her *The Girl in Room 222.*"

"It's *The Girl in Suite 23.*"

"What's the worst that could happen? You add another row to your rejection spreadsheet?"

"That spreadsheet is a valuable data analysis tool," Leigh protested, but she felt her resolve weakening. Maybe it was the late hour, or the way Ami's concern felt heavier than usual.

"Fine," Ami said. "Talk to that agent, and this weekend I'll help you brainstorm Instagram ideas for funeral insurance or whatever depressing product Sharon's pushing."

Leigh gathered her bag, already mentally rehearsing tomorrow's presentation. "Deal. But if this ends in rejection number forty-nine, you're buying the drinks next month."

"Deal." Ami stood, her sketchbook disappearing into her oversized bag.

They stepped out into the night, the neon signs of the Half Door painting them in shades of possibility. Leigh's phone buzzed again—probably Sharon again seeing if she could push the meeting to 6 a.m.—but for once, she let it ring.

four

· · ·

Authenticity Issues

LEIGH'S CURSOR hovered over the Gmail refresh button for the thirty-ninth time that morning. Three weeks, four days, and approximately seven hours since she'd sent her manuscript to Mila Clark at the Clark Literary Agency. Not that she was counting.

"—and with these Medicare supplement numbers—" Sharon's voice cut through the fog of Leigh's inbox obsession. "Leigh? Are you with us?"

"Sorry, could you repeat the question?" Leigh minimized her email, grateful that her laptop screen faced away from the conference table. The familiar graphs and charts of her quarterly presentation stared back at her, a maze of metrics and conversion rates that should have commanded her full attention.

The morning crawled by in fifteen-minute increments, each one marked by another check of her inbox. The rejection spreadsheet sat open in another tab, waiting for row forty-nine.

"You know what they say about watched inboxes." Dawn appeared at Leigh's desk just as she was contemplating a strategic lunch-at-desk email-monitoring session. "Come on, the break room has actual human beings in it. And fewer opportunities for refresh-button repetitive stress injury."

The break room smelled of burnt coffee and microwaved leftovers, but at least it offered distance from her laptop. Leigh picked at her salad while Dawn launched into a story about her daughter's latest school drama.

"—and then Madison told the principal that the dress code was a tool of the patriarchy, which I blame entirely on that feminist theory book she found in my office—" Dawn paused mid-anecdote. "You're not hearing a word I'm saying, are you?"

"Madison. Patriarchy. Dress code." Leigh's phone lit up with a missed call notification. Her stomach dropped as she saw the 212 area code and the waiting voicemail. Three weeks of obsessively checking her phone, and of course Dawn's sister would call during the one meeting she couldn't excuse herself from. "I have to—"

"Check it," Dawn nudged her.

Leigh's fingers trembled slightly as she pressed play. Mila Clark's voice emerged from the phone, warm but professional: "Hello, Leigh. This is Mila Clark from Clark Literary. I'd love to discuss your manuscript when you have a moment. You can reach me at this number."

"It's your sister," Leigh whispered, her heart somewhere in the vicinity of her sensible heels. "She wants me to call her back."

"Go! Use the small conference room on six." Dawn gathered Leigh's salad and pushed it toward the break room fridge. "The AC's broken but at least it's private. No one will hear you hyperventilate."

The elevator ride to the sixth floor lasted approximately three lifetimes. Leigh's reflection in the polished doors looked surprisingly calm for someone whose entire future balanced on the edge of a phone call. Her fingers shook slightly as she dialed the New York number.

"Leigh Dolan?" The voice on the other end carried the same warm professionalism from the voicemail, which Leigh instantly envied. "Thank you for calling back so quickly. I hope I'm not catching you at a bad time?"

"Not at all." Leigh paced the small conference room, watching Hartford's skyline shimmer. "I'm just between meetings." The lie felt professional, practiced.

"I wanted to chat with you about *The Girl in Suite 23*. Thank you again for sending it my way—I appreciate you trusting me with your work." Mila's tone stayed warm, but Leigh recognized the rhythm of rejection building in her cadence. "Your prose is sharp, the pacing is well-managed, and you clearly have a gift for creating compelling characters."

Here it comes.

"Unfortunately," Mila continued, "the current market for domestic suspense is…saturated. Especially books with 'Girl' in the title. Publishers are looking for something fresh."

The broken AC had turned the room into a stifling box. Leigh sank into a faux-leather chair, the vinyl sticking to her thighs. In the window's reflection, she watched her image blur, a fleeting echo, much like Miranda trapped in that sterile hospital corridor.

"Listen, I don't normally do this," Mila said, her tone shifting, "but my sister speaks very highly of you. And I see real potential in your voice, your storytelling. I believe you have a future as a published author—"

"Thank you," Leigh managed, her fingers already twitching to update her rejection spreadsheet.

"Have you ever considered paranormal romance?"

The question hung in the stifling air.

"I'm sorry?" Had the heat finally gotten to her?

"Specifically, LGBTQ+ witch fiction. It's booming right now, and your ability to balance immersive description with emotional resonance could really shine in that space."

Leigh stared at her reflection. A horrifying thought struck her—had Dawn somehow given her sister the wrong impression about Leigh's personal life?

"I don't...I mean, I'm not..." She took a breath, trying to organize her thoughts with her usual precision. "I write realistic fiction. I don't know anything about witchcraft, and—"

"I know it might sound like an odd suggestion," Mila said. "But in my experience, talented novelists can write in almost any genre. If you're serious about pursuing this as a career, it might be worth exploring something different."

"But wouldn't there be...authenticity issues with the LGBT stuff?" Leigh pressed, her marketing brain already cataloging potential problems. "I'm not part of that community. Wouldn't that be—"

"We could always use sensitivity readers," Mila cut in smoothly. "It's standard practice these days. But we're getting ahead of ourselves. The important thing is finding your voice in a market that's actually buying. And right now, that market loves witches falling in love with other witches."

Leigh's mind spun with the surreal turn of the conversation. "Witch fiction?" she repeated weakly.

"Send me anything you write in that genre," Mila said. "I'm serious. I'd love to see it. Just...maybe skip the 'Girl' titles?"

THE CONFERENCE ROOM felt smaller than usual as Leigh hung up the phone. Hartford's spring rain pressed against the windows, turning the city into a blur of gray possibility. Her laptop waited on her desk downstairs, the rejection spreadsheet a monument to practical failure.

"How'd it go?" Dawn ambushed her at the elevator, concern etched across her features.

"Your sister thinks I should write witch romance. Gay

witch romance." The words sounded even more absurd out loud. "Is this some kind of elaborate practical joke?"

"Mila doesn't joke about market trends." Dawn's eyes lit up. "She offered to read more of your work?"

"If I write it. Which I won't." The elevator arrived with a cheerful ding that felt oddly inappropriate. "I don't know anything about witches. Or romance."

Back at her desk, Leigh opened the spreadsheet that tracked her literary failures. The cursor blinked in the "Rejection Reason" column of row forty-nine. She typed "Market over—" then stopped, deleting the letters one by one. She hesitated over the keyboard before typing simply: "Wrong genre?"

The afternoon dissolved into a series of meetings that required her physical presence but not her attention. Brad from Digital Optimization droned on about engagement metrics while Leigh peeked at her phone on her lap, diving into a world she never thought she'd explore.

"*Spells and Cupcakes,*" she muttered, scrolling through Amazon's paranormal romance bestsellers. "*The Witch's Girlfriend. Cauldron of Love.*" Each title felt more ridiculous than the last.

That evening at the Half Door, Leigh recounted the whole surreal conversation to Ami over their usual Thursday cocktails. She expected sympathy, maybe even shared outrage at the suggestion that she abandon her carefully crafted suspense novel for… whatever this was.

Instead, Ami burst out laughing, the sound carrying across their corner table. "This is literally perfect," she gasped, gesturing between them. "We've been practicing gay romance every Thursday for years!"

"That's different. That's just our thing. And it's not real." Leigh took a long sip of her drink. "Besides, it's not the romance part I'm worried about. It's the witch thing. I write realistic fiction. Murder mysteries. Thrillers. Evil husbands.

Kidnapped women. Amnesia. Not…magic spells and talking cats."

"Oh my god, listen to this." Ami pulled out her phone, her voice taking on an exaggerated dramatic tone. *"When Sophie discovers she's a witch, her carefully ordered life turns upside down. But the biggest spell of all might be the one cast by her mysterious new neighbor…"* She scrolled further. "Four point nine stars. *The photocopying scene was surprisingly hot.*"

"The what scene?"

"See? It's like they wrote it specifically for you."

A man in a polo shirt that screamed "just got off my shift at the investment firm downtown" approached their table, drink in hand. Without missing a beat, Ami slid her arm around Leigh's shoulders. "Sorry, we're celebrating our anniversary.

"Research," Ami whispered as he retreated. "You're basically doing field work right now."

Leigh pulled out her phone, finding the books Ami had mentioned. Her Amazon cart filled with titles she never thought she'd own: *The Sweet Shop Spell, Checks, Hexes, and Exes, Love Under the Cinnamon Moon.*

The waiter dropped off their check, and Leigh noticed she'd been doodling in her planner's margins. Tiny broomsticks and cauldrons surrounded tomorrow's meeting notes. For the first time since Mila's call, something shifted in her chest—not quite excitement, but maybe the possibility of it.

"You know what this means, right?" Ami's grin turned wicked. "We need to step up our fake dating game. For research purposes, of course."

"Whatever." Leigh hit "Buy Now" on her phone, watching her carefully curated Amazon algorithm cry in confusion.

five

. . .

I Want That Person to Be You

LEIGH'S LIVING room wall had transformed into something between a detective's murder board and a doctoral thesis on witch romance novels. Post-it notes in a rainbow of colors created a tapestry of literary analysis: green for magic systems (wayfinding crystals required, wands optional), pink for romance beats (first kiss by 30% mark, all-is-lost moment at 75%), yellow for worldbuilding rules (no casting spells on first dates, familiars are basically furry therapists).

Her coffee table disappeared beneath stacks of library books with titles like *A Cultural History of Witchcraft* and *Modern Wiccan Practices*. A half-empty wine glass balanced precariously on *Love Spells Through the Ages*, leaving a ring on the cover that the Hartford Public Library would definitely notice.

The spreadsheet open on her laptop tracked everything from average chapter length to spells-per-scene ratios. Column K analyzed the correlation between magical power levels and romantic tension. Column L tracked familiar species by popularity (cats won by a significant margin, followed by ravens and, inexplicably, hedgehogs).

"I might be overthinking this," Leigh muttered to her own

reflection in the darkened window. The city lights beyond the glass offered no argument.

☂

THE NEXT MORNING's team brainstorming session blurred the lines between her research and reality. Brad from Digital Optimization's suggestion about viral marketing reminded her suspiciously of a love potion gone wrong in *The Bad Girl's Midnight Coven Book Club*. She caught herself color-coding meeting notes: green for actionable items (practical magic), pink for aspirational goals (wishful thinking), yellow for budget constraints (curses in disguise).

"Leigh?" Sharon's voice cut through her categorization of Ted from Accounting's PowerPoint abilities (definitely a hedge witch). "Could you stay late today? I'd like to discuss some changes in the department coming up."

"Uh, sure…" The words "changes in the department" carried the same ominous weight as "unfortunately, in the current market." Leigh's stomach twisted as she imagined all the possibilities—budget cuts, restructuring, or worse, a transfer to Sales. The thought of cold-calling potential clients about Medicare supplements made her current job feel like a writer's retreat.

By six o'clock, she found herself in the corner office, watching the April rain trace patterns on the window and calculating how many months of rent her emergency fund would cover.

Sharon settled into her ergonomic chair. The wall behind her was lined with industry awards and certifications—a corporate trophy case that seemed to watch Leigh with judging eyes.

"We're making some changes to the department structure," Sharon began, shuffling papers on her desk in that particular way that meant bad news was coming. "Marketing and Communications are being consolidated into a single group."

Leigh's fingers found the edge of her chair, gripping the metal frame. *Consolidated. Streamlined. Optimized.* All the sanitized corporate words for cutting jobs. She'd seen this before at her last company—first came the meetings about synergy, then the cardboard boxes.

"Some positions will be eliminated," Sharon continued, and Leigh's mind raced to her monthly budget. She could cut out her Netflix, maybe sublease her parking spot—

"Barry is leaving us."

Leigh blinked. Barry, the Communications Director, whose main contribution seemed to be forwarding emails with "Thoughts?" in the subject line.

"We need someone to step up as Senior Marketing Manager," Sharon said, leaning forward. "Someone to oversee all the creatives in both departments. Someone who understands the big picture." She paused, her eyes fixed on Leigh. "I want that person to be you."

The words took a moment to process. "Me?"

"You're dedicated, reliable, and you have the strategic mindset we need." Sharon's smile was genuine, the kind she usually reserved for client wins. "There's a significant salary increase, of course. New office. Though I should mention the hours will be longer, especially as we sort out the new department."

The promotion dangled before her. More money meant more security, but more hours meant less time for writing. Less time staring at that cursor, true, but also less time for the stories that kept trying to escape her corporate cage.

"Thank you," Leigh said, trying to keep her voice steady. "This is... I'm honored. Would it be okay if I took the weekend to think it over?" The words tasted responsible, professional—exactly what a future Senior Marketing Manager should say when offered a promotion, rather than what she was actually thinking: *I'm about to sacrifice my novel on the altar of corporate advancement.*

Sharon's expression softened into something almost maternal. "Take the weekend," she said, standing to signal the end of their meeting. "But Leigh? Don't doubt yourself. I've watched you handle every challenge we've thrown at you. You're ready for this step."

Ready to give up on everything else, Leigh thought, but she managed a polite smile as she gathered her things. The rain had stopped outside Sharon's window, leaving the glass streaked with trails that looked like prison bars in the office lights.

BACK IN HER APARTMENT, Leigh retreated to the balcony with her laptop and wine. The small concrete space had morphed from occasional smoking sanctuary into full writing refuge. She added "workplace tension" to her spreadsheet column of witch romance conflicts, wondering what Ami would say about Sharon's offer. Probably something cutting and perfect that would end up as dialogue in the book.

Her phone buzzed—Ami herself, no doubt hiding in the art room between conferences with parents who couldn't understand why their precious angels weren't all instant Picassos.

How's the research going?

Through the window Leigh snapped a photo of her Post-it covered wall and sent it. The reply came almost instantly.

You've gone full Beautiful Mind.

The wine glass beside her laptop had reached that perfect

level of empty that justified either stopping or opening another bottle. Leigh chose option B—if she was going to write about witches falling in love with other witches, she needed chemical assistance. Her attempts so far read like market research reports with spells: "Subject A encounters Subject B in a magical bookstore (settings spreadsheet, row 147) and experiences immediate attraction (romance beat checklist, item 3)."

Every time she opened a blank document, her mind filled with charts instead of stories. Her latest spreadsheet tracked magical objects across twelve different series, color-coded by their relevance to plot development. The Latin dictionary on her coffee table had more Post-it flags than pages. She'd even created a pivot table analyzing the correlation between spell complexity and romantic tension, as if that would somehow make writing about love—especially this kind of love—feel less foreign.

When she finally forced herself to write a scene, she spent forty-five minutes cross-referencing her "Common Witch Powers by Chapter Introduction" chart before letting her protagonist cast a single spell. Two paragraphs and three hours later, she had a scene that read like a workplace policy for supernatural mishaps.

Around midnight, back on the couch inside and deep in her fifth glass of wine, Leigh stared at her attempts to write. The words felt as hollow as her marketing presentations. She couldn't connect with these characters—their magical lives, their instant attractions, their perfect understanding of who they were and what they wanted. Her own romantic history consisted of one failed marriage, three semi-serious relationships, and a series of forgettable first dates. All with dudes. What did she know about soul-deep connections or earth-shattering passion?

She stood up, swaying slightly, and looked at her wall of Post-its. She'd turned creativity into a data point, approaching romance like it was a Medicare Advantage campaign. No wonder her attempts at writing felt about as magical as a quarterly earnings report. Maybe Mila was wrong. Maybe she should stick to writing about what she knew. Normal people doing normal things, like getting divorced and failing at their dreams.

Leigh slumped back onto her couch, leaving her notes on the wall as evidence of another failed attempt at reinvention. Her laptop screen glowed accusingly, cursor blinking at the start of yet another unfinished scene. Monday she'd tell Sharon yes to the promotion. At least spreadsheets made sense.

six

. . .

Virginia Slims & Romance Novels

SATURDAY MORNING ARRIVED with the special kind of headache reserved for wine-soaked regrets. Leigh's laptop screen reflected a museum installation of empty glasses on her coffee table, a tribute to poor life choices and failed creativity. She highlighted everything she'd written over the past week—five separate attempts at witch romance, none making it past chapter three—and hit delete. The blank document looked better than her forced attempts at magical meet-cutes and supernatural sexual tension.

Her phone buzzed. Noah's name appeared on the screen, triggering the familiar mix of guilt and irritation that characterized their post-divorce communications.

> **Need to talk about the desk. Ellie's moving in**
> **next weekend and we're redoing the garage**

The antique writing desk. Her grandmother's pride and joy, now trapped in Noah's garage like some furniture-based metaphor for her life. Leigh surveyed her cramped one-bedroom apartment, already overstuffed with the spoils of their divided life. The desk had been the one thing she'd truly wanted, but between her collection of moderately priced IKEA furniture and the books that seemed to breed on every surface, there wasn't even room for false hope.

> I know. Working on a space for it

Noah's response came quickly:

> You've been working on it for months. We
> need it out of here

> Maybe if you hadn't rushed into moving in
> with someone you've known for 5 min, we'd
> have more time to figure this out

Leigh hit send before her better judgment could intervene.

> At least I'm moving forward with my life

The text stung with the particular sharpness of truth wrapped in cruelty. Leigh's thumbs moved faster than her common sense.

> Well, I'm sure Ellie's Pinterest-perfect
> decorating style will really brighten up the
> place. Nothing says domestic bliss like
> mass-produced farmhouse chic and live
> laugh love signs

She dropped her phone onto the couch and walked to the kitchen, where an unopened bottle of wine stood sentinel next to her coffee maker. Should she crack it open? The wall clock read 10:47 a.m.—practically noon, which was practically evening in failure-to-launch writer time.

Her laptop waited patiently as she refilled her coffee mug instead. The blank document somehow looked even blanker than before. She managed three paragraphs about a witch discovering her powers in a small rural town that felt suspiciously like *Heartland* with pentagrams.

Marianne stared at the spell book, its ancient pages promising secrets of love and destiny. With trembling fingers, she traced the Latin words, feeling the magic spark beneath her skin. Perhaps this time, the right incantation would finally—

"God, this is garbage," Leigh muttered, highlighting the text. Her finger hovered over the delete key, then moved to her research spreadsheet. All those hours of analysis, color-coding, and pattern recognition. She'd treated writing like a marketing campaign, as if she could A/B test her way to creativity.

The delete key clicked with surprising satisfaction. The spreadsheet vanished, taking with it her carefully curated tables of magical objects, her romance beat analysis, and her color-coded guide to witch-appropriate nomenclature. Her wall of Post-its stared back at her, a paper monument to everything she was trying and failing to be.

Her phone buzzed. Noah again.

> Just let me know what you want to do with the desk ASAP. If you can't take it, I'll drop it at Goodwill

The suggestion hit like a slap. That desk had been her grandmother's sanctuary, the place where she'd written letters and balanced checkbooks and created the illusion of order in a chaotic world. The idea of it being sold to some stranger who'd probably paint it chalk white and distress it to match their farmhouse aesthetic made Leigh's chest tight.

She took another sip of coffee, remembering the way her grandmother's perfume had lingered in the desk's drawers, how the wood felt smooth and warm under small hands. The memory collided with her current reality: an overworked divorced chick trying to write gay witch romance while living in furniture purgatory.

The cursor blinked on her screen, as judgmental as Sharon's Mont Blanc pen tapping against quarterly reports. Leigh closed her laptop. She'd lost her grandmother's desk, her marriage, and now apparently her ability to write anything that didn't read like a supernatural marketing strategy.

Leigh reached for her phone. She scrolled past Sharon's number (two missed texts about the new department) and Noah's thread (radio silence after the Goodwill threat) to land on Ami.

"I'm having an existential crisis," Leigh announced when Ami picked up. "Noah's going to send Grandma Margaret's desk to Goodwill, I can't write a single believable sentence about witches falling in love, and I'm pretty sure I'm going to end up as one of those corporate zombies who dies clutching a PowerPoint presentation about social media engagement metrics."

"Sounds like a normal weekend for you," Ami replied. The background music blaring suggested she was at her studio—probably working on another one of her big abstract paintings that made Leigh's apartment feel like a beige cavern of mediocrity. "Wait, Noah's doing what with the desk?"

"Trying to get rid of it." The words tasted bitter. "They're 'redoing' the garage into a craft room for Ellie, which apparently means getting rid of my furniture. I don't have room for it here, but I can't—" Her voice caught. "I used to do my homework at that desk while my grandmother read. She kept her good stationery in the top left drawer and had this secret compartment in the back that she thought nobody knew about."

"You never told me about that."

"Family secret."

"What was in it?"

"Virginia Slims and romance novels." Leigh laughed, the sound catching in her throat. "The really trashy ones with Fabio on the cover. She would have hated what I'm writing now. Not because it's gay—she would have been fine with that. Because it's so…bland and fake."

The silence on the other end stretched just long enough for Leigh to contemplate hanging up and opening up that wine. Then Ami spoke: "Maybe that's your problem. You're trying to write about witches without knowing any actual witches."

"I've done the research—"

"On your computer," Ami said. "You know what? Salem's like two hours away. The literal Witch Capital of the World. They must have real witches there, right? Among all the tourist trap stuff?"

Leigh snorted. "Right. I'll just drive to Salem and ask around for authentic witches. 'Excuse me, do you happen to know any real spell-casters who'd like to beta read my romantic witch novel?'"

"Why not? It's better than sitting in your apartment, staring at the walls."

"I'll have you know I've been staring at spreadsheets—"

"Go be a tourist, stay overnight, maybe find some inspiration that isn't color-coded."

The suggestion should have seemed ridiculous. But after she hung up with Ami, Leigh found herself on her laptop, scrolling through hotel options in Salem. The historic Hawthorne Hotel had some last-minute rooms available—apparently not everyone planned their witch-hunting expeditions six months before Halloween. The nightly rate made her cringe, but if she ended up taking the promotion, she could probably manage it.

Leigh's cursor hovered over the "confirm reservation" button. On her kitchen counter, a small forest of mail awaited her attention, including a notice about her lease renewal (due in two months), and a final warning about her parking permit (expired last week). All the mundane responsibilities of a sensible adult life.

To hell with it. She clicked "confirm."

The packing process proved surprisingly easy, probably because her brain had reduced it to another data set: two business casual outfits (in case she spilled road trip food on herself), one pair of comfortable walking shoes (practical), her laptop (essential), and the notebook where she'd been tracking witch romance tropes (now repurposed for actual observations). She added her good umbrella as a concession to the New England spring weather, which treated rain as less of a meteorological event and more of a personal philosophy.

Standing in her bedroom, overnight bag packed and propped against the door, Leigh realized this was the first genuinely impulsive thing she'd done since signing her divorce papers. Even then, she'd made a pros and cons list first. Her grandmother would have approved—Margaret Dolan's secret romance collection had been built on the principle that sometimes you needed to escape your own story to figure out what kind of book you were really in.

The desk could stay in Noah's garage a little longer. Ellie's Pinterest-perfect plans for domestic bliss would have to accommodate one family heirloom for a few more days. Right now, Leigh needed to find something real to write about, even if she had to drive to Massachusetts to find it.

On the way out of her apartment, Leigh caught her reflection in the mirror by the door: a slightly disheveled marketing manager with the wild eyes of someone about to either make a huge mistake or have an actual adventure. She couldn't tell which yet, but for the first time in weeks, she felt something that her data analysis hadn't predicted: hope.

seven

. . .

So What Brings You to Salem?

BY 2:30 THAT AFTERNOON, Leigh was standing in line at the Salem Witch Museum, surrounded by tourists in "My Other Ride Is A Broomstick" t-shirts bought three blocks away.

The museum's entrance fee equaled roughly four drinks at the Half Door, but she'd committed to this research expedition. The teenage ticket taker barely glanced up from her phone as she waved Leigh through to join the next tour group. Inside, life-sized dioramas loomed in dramatic spotlighting, while a narrator with the gravitas of a 1950s documentary intoned facts about spectral evidence and mass hysteria.

"Notice the authentic period clothing," the scratchy recording droned, as Leigh studied a decidedly inauthentic-looking mannequin meant to represent Tituba. Her phone's notes app was open, but she'd only managed to type "period costumes = polyester?" and "why does every accused witch have the same face?" The professional part of her brain couldn't help critiquing the presentation—this place desperately needed a focus group and a brand refresh.

After an hour of dated exhibits and gift shop witchcraft, she'd had enough.

Essex Street was a tourist trap nightmare. Giggling teenagers paraded past, their shopping bags swinging with purchased authenticity: crystal balls made in China, mass-produced spell books, pentagram necklaces that would probably turn their wearers' necks green by dinner. She passed the bronze statue of Samantha Stevens from "Bewitched," its metal nose polished bright by countless tourist touches. The only thing she added to her notes app was a half-hearted attempt to describe a street vendor's "genuine witch's potion" (red Gatorade with floating gummy worms, $7.99).

The Witch House offered no relief, with its tour guide in a questionably accurate Puritan costume explaining the significance of seventeenth-century architectural features to a crowd more interested in their phones than history. Leigh dutifully noted details about ceiling beams and window placements, but her heart wasn't in it.

"And this would have been the parlor," the guide announced, gesturing to a room furnished with heavy wooden pieces that reminded Leigh uncomfortably of Grandma Margaret's desk, still hostage in Noah's garage. "Note the writing desk by the window—it's a reproduction, but accurate to the period."

Leigh studied the desk, its dark wood gleaming with careful restoration. Would her grandmother's desk end up in some museum someday, with tourists filing past while a guide explained the significance of its secret compartment? (Margaret would have hated that—she'd taken her hidden romance collection seriously).

Finally, the Old Burying Point Cemetery offered blessed silence after the commercial chaos. Here, under centuries-old trees, the weight of history felt almost tangible. The April wind scattered dead leaves across gravestones worn soft by time and weather. Leigh traced her fingers over the carved skull symbols.

At the adjacent Witch Trials Memorial, simple stone benches bore the names of the accused. No gift shops, no cartoon witches, just stark testimony to human cruelty and courage. Leigh sat on the cool stone, phone forgotten in her bag. A plaque quoted Bridget Bishop's final words: "I am no witch. I am innocent. I know nothing of it." The fluffy witch romance plots she'd been forcing suddenly felt not just inadequate but disrespectful.

Outside, the afternoon sun cast long shadows across cobblestones that had definitely been installed during the last decade. Leigh checked her museum-provided walking map, now creased and coffee-stained. She had time for one more attraction before dinner. The House of the Seven Gables was open for fifteen more minutes, though it was clear across town and had nothing to do with witches. At this point, that felt like a selling point. But instead, she trudged back along Essex Street towards her hotel.

A text from Ami lit up her phone:

Found any real witches yet?

Leigh glanced around at the tourist circus: the tarot readers setting up card tables for the evening crowd, the shops selling "authentic" spell components, the street performers in pointy hats posing for photos.

Unless they're hiding behind the snow globe display at Salem Witch Museum Gift Shop 3, I'm thinking no.

Keep looking. Maybe try somewhere less obvious?

Less obvious seemed impossible in Salem, where every

brick and doorway had been branded, packaged, and priced for maximum supernatural appeal. Leigh tucked her phone away and headed toward the hotel, leaving the witch-themed commerce behind. Maybe she'd try to hit the House of the Seven Gables in the morning. At least Nathaniel Hawthorne had never tried to write a romance about queer witches discovering their powers through love. Though given what she'd learned about Puritan furniture today, maybe she should consider a novel about an enchanted writing desk instead.

THE GROWL in her stomach finally won out over her desire to hide in the hotel room with mini-bar peanuts and whatever was left of her writerly dignity. A massive tavern and steakhouse loomed over Essex Street, its windows glowing with what looked like enough ambient light to power a small city. Of course, Salem would have the restaurant equivalent of a theme park—the carved wooden sign even featured a witch riding a T-bone steak instead of a broomstick.

Inside, the cacophony of tourist chatter and clinking glasses reverberated off exposed brick walls and prefab rough-hewn ceiling beams. The hostess, wearing what appeared to be a historically inaccurate corset over her polo shirt, directed Leigh toward one of the three separate bars. Because apparently a single bar couldn't handle the crushing need for Salem-themed cocktails with names like "The Hanging Judge" and "Black Cat's Revenge."

But the far corner of the rightmost bar offered unexpected sanctuary: a high-top table partially hidden behind a support beam, with a clear view of both the exits and the local crowd that had carved out their own territory away from the tourist zones. The bartender here moved with the efficient grace of someone who'd mastered the art of appearing busy enough to discourage small talk while still noticing empty glasses.

Leigh settled in with her wine (house cab, perfectly adequate) and notebook (spiral doodles already spreading across the margins). The tavern's menu managed to avoid witch puns entirely, and the burger actually tasted like real food instead of gift shop novelty. She found herself relaxing into the festive noise, the way the locals at the bar navigated around the tourists with practiced ease, the simple pleasure of anonymity in a crowded room.

A man sitting alone two tables away caught her eye and smiled—one of those practiced smiles that suggested he'd workshopped it in corporate training seminars. In her normal life, she would have buried herself in her phone or fabricated an urgent email to answer.

But this wasn't her normal life. Normal Leigh was back in Hartford, writing sensible emails about accepting promotions and crafting careful responses to Noah about furniture logistics. This Leigh—the one who'd booked a last-minute hotel room and fled to Salem—had different ideas about risk management.

The man picked up on her smile and sauntered over. "Looks like you could use a refill," the man said, gesturing to her empty glass. His blue button-down screamed business casual, but his loosened tie suggested he was off duty. He wasn't quite old enough to be her dad, but definitely old enough to be her uncle. She didn't care.

"Actually," Leigh heard herself say, "I wouldn't mind something a little more potent." The words tasted like rebellion on her tongue.

His eyebrows lifted appreciatively. "Now, that's what I like to hear. Be right back." He returned approximately ninety seconds later with two shots of Patron. Dude worked fast.

His name was Matt, and he sold medical devices to hospitals—the kind of ordinary job that made her marketing career look exotic by comparison. After a day of dodging tourist trap witchcraft and overpriced "authentic" spell books, talking about sales quotas and product demos felt refreshingly normal. The tequila didn't hurt either, transforming her usual overthinking into a pleasant buzz that made relocating to the bar seem like the most logical decision she'd made all weekend.

"So what brings you to Salem?" he asked, signaling the bartender for another round.

Leigh considered her options. She could tell him about her failed attempts at writing supernatural romance, her grandmother's endangered desk, her ex-husband's girl-friend's Pinterest boards. Instead, she said, "Just playing tourist."

The conversation meandered through safe topics: their jobs (his involved quarterly sales targets, hers was "in marketing"), their thoughts on Salem (touristy but lively), whether the band in the corner was trying too hard (definitely).

Ninety minutes (and three more rounds of Patron) later, they stumbled into his hotel room at the Hampton Inn. The room offered all the ambiance of an airport terminal, but it had the distinct advantage of not being haunted by either actual ghosts or her own creative failures.

"Want something to keep the party going?" Matt asked, pulling a prescription bottle from his bag. "Perks of knowing doctors," he added with a wink. "Totally safe. Just like a Red Bull, but in pill form."

Leigh studied the orange bottle, thinking about all her sensible rules, all her careful planning, all the spreadsheets and analyses that had failed to produce anything worth keep-ing. The whole situation screamed *bad decision*, but then again, so did writing witch romance novels and running away to Salem.

"I like Red Bull," she said, accepting the pill he offered.

What was one more reckless choice in a weekend full of them?

In the artificial dark of blackout curtains, Matt became a collection of unremarkable movements and fumbling urgency. His cologne smelled expensive but forgettable, like him. The pill kept her uncomfortably alert through what turned out to be perfunctory sex, leaving her to wonder why she wasn't enjoying it more after all that tequila. When they tried again later, she found herself counting the water stains on the ceiling, bored despite the chemical buzz still humming through her veins.

Leigh closed her eyes and thought about all the romance novels her grandmother had hidden in that desk. None of them had chapters like this—anonymous hotel rooms and pharmaceuticals and the dawning realization that she'd rather be anywhere else.

Margaret Dolan's heroines always found earth-shattering love in windswept locations. They never had to write their own stories or figure out where to store family heirlooms or lie still in the dark, pretending to sleep until their one-night stand's breathing turned to snores so they could gather their clothes and slip away.

The hallway carpet muffled her steps, its geometric pattern swimming slightly in her still-fuzzy vision. In the elevator, she checked her phone: one missed call from Ami, but nothing from Noah about the desk.

Salem was just waking up when Leigh slipped out of Matt's hotel room, the delivery trucks already double-parked as they restocked the endless gift shops with mass-produced magic. Her own hotel was less than a ten-minute walk away, so soon she crawled into her bed, still buzzing uncomfortably from whatever had been in that pill.

Three hours of restless dozing later, she was feeling no better. Her room at had transformed from quaint to suffocating sometime during her fitful sleep. The notebook on the bedside table still contained nothing but doodles and half-formed observations about tourist trap aesthetics. She'd come to Salem looking for authenticity and found only gift shops and a sad hook-up. Even the shadows seemed to mock her ill-fated pilgrimage for inspiration.

The front desk clerk barely looked up as Leigh checked out. "Was everything satisfactory with your stay?"

The question felt like the final insult in a weekend of mounting humiliations. Right now, all Leigh wanted was to be in her car, heading back to Connecticut, putting as much distance as possible between herself and this monument to manufactured mysticism.

"Perfect," Leigh replied instead, her voice on autopilot. "Very authentic."

She tossed her Salem tourist map in the brass lobby trash can, where it landed among coffee cups and empty snack bags from the vending machine. The map's cover promised "Real Magic!" in a font that managed to be both gothic and desperately eager to please.

Leigh surrendered to reality: she was done with witches, done chasing impossible dreams, done pretending she could write her way out of her perfectly adequate life. Time to focus on what she was actually good at—maybe that promotion wouldn't be so bad. Insurance could be creative, right? She almost laughed at the thought. Maybe she'd take up quilting instead; at least then she'd have something to show for her efforts besides a recycling bin full of rejection letters.

Another missed call from Ami lit up her phone screen. Leigh let it go to voicemail, her stomach clenching at the thought of explaining her failed research trip to her best friend. How exactly did you tell someone that their well-meaning suggestion to find inspiration had led to pills and a stranger's hotel room?

eight

. . .

Wilma's

THE HANGOVER CAUGHT up with Leigh just past Salem, each mile marker on I-95 pulsing against her temples. By South Lynnfield, the stabs of pain were pounding in time with every "should" that had been running through her head since last night—should have stuck to wine, should have stayed in her own hotel room, should have said no to the Red Bull pills, should have never gone to Salem in the first place.

When the exit sign for the next town materialized through her windshield's glare, she knew she needed industrial-strength caffeine if she was going to survive the drive back to Hartford.

Past a sign that read "Entering Reading. Est. 1639," Main Street unfolded before her like a lifestyle magazine's idea of small-town New England, all brick-faced low-rises with the kind of calculated charm that attracted young professionals fleeing Boston prices.

She crawled past the expected parade of businesses: a comic book store advertising a Magic: The Gathering tournament, one of those upscale tattoo parlors (which held as much interest for her as the comic book store, making her feel both ancient and oddly pedestrian for having resisted the urge to get inked), a Pilates studio where lean women in coordinated athleisure stretched on reformer machines, and the inevitable Dunkin' that was her backup plan if she couldn't find something more appealing.

She finally wedged her Kia Soul in front of what appeared to be an artisanal pet grooming boutique, noting the parking signs with their byzantine schedule of restrictions (because of course a town this quaint would have a doctorate-level parking enforcement system).

A movement caught her eye as she stepped onto the sidewalk. A homeless man stood near the corner, tall and heavyset, with a gray beard that looked like it had been growing for decades. His coat appeared to have been assembled from the remains of every leather jacket that had died in Reading since 1975. The overall effect suggested a grizzly bear that had been adopted by the Hell's Angels.

Leigh reached for her wallet, remembering how her grandmother used to say that kindness given was never wasted. She held out a twenty, wondering if she was being practical or just trying to bank some karmic credit after last night's choices.

"Merci. Votre chemin croise aujourd'hui la fortune," the man said, following with another stream of rapid French that sent Leigh's mind scrambling back to her two semesters of college language requirements. She had no idea what he said, but his accent sounded perfect to her untrained ear. It briefly made her question her assumptions about homeless French speakers in Massachusetts suburbs.

She wandered down Main Street, her headache conducting a symphony behind her eyes. The storefronts offered more of the usual small-town mix: a real estate office advertising historic homes at modern prices, a boutique that seemed to sell both artisanal candles and local honey, and a shop dedicated entirely to decorative lawn flags. Then, tucked away on a side street, she spotted it—a coffee shop in a converted colonial house. An antique wooden sign identified it as "Wilma's," complete with a hand-painted steaming coffee cup.

The bell above the door chimed as Leigh stepped inside, the sound piercing her tender consciousness. The interior unfolded like someone's eccentric great-aunt's living room after a lifetime of careful hoarding: maps covered the walls, books crammed every shelf, and various knick-knacks occupied every horizontal surface. Games, greeting cards, and local artwork competed for space with calendars and souvenir coffee mugs. The whole place had the cluttered comfort of a room that had grown organically rather than been designed by committee.

As her eyes adjusted to the dim lighting, Leigh spotted the coffee counter tucked into the back corner. A pastry case displayed an array of baked goods that seemed genuinely homemade rather than carefully styled to appear homemade. Half a dozen mismatched tables dotted the space, most occupied by people just hanging out.

A chalkboard sign propped on the counter declared, "Yes! We Have Cold Brew!" in enthusiastic handwriting. Leigh ordered one, then noticed a tray of chocolate cupcakes in the case. Her grandmother's voice echoed in her memory: sugar and caffeine cure most sins. She added a cupcake to her order, choosing to interpret her hangover as a sin in need of curing.

The barista worked with quiet efficiency, no corporate-mandated small talk or forced cheerfulness. Leigh found a small table beneath a bulletin board that documented the community's entire social calendar in layers of overlapping flyers. She scrolled through her phone while nibbling the cupcake. For the first time since waking up in Matt's hotel room, the world felt marginally less hostile.

Deep in her texts—another message from Noah about the desk—she barely registered the presence beside her table until a soft voice broke through her concentration. "Excuse me, I just need to get in behind you."

Leigh glanced up from her phone just long enough to see the back of a young woman holding a stack of flyers inching toward the bulletin board. She shifted her chair forward, muttering an apology for blocking the way, her attention already drifting back to Noah's latest passive-aggressive update about storage fees.

The movement in her peripheral vision continued as the woman tried to maneuver in the tight space between Leigh's chair and the wall. A flash of pink-streaked blonde hair crossed her field of vision, but Leigh kept her eyes fixed on her phone, maintaining that polite bubble of personal space that New Englanders had elevated to an art form.

"Thanks." The woman turned, and their eyes met. The world tilted sideways. An electric current raced through Leigh's body, the sensation both foreign and somehow achingly familiar. Reality blurred at the edges, the coffee shop's cluttered walls dissolving into watercolor smears. For one terrifying moment, a single thought crystallized with impossible clarity: *I'm not who I think I am.*

Panic clawed at her chest. Was this a stroke? Some delayed reaction to Matt's Red Bull pill? The room spun like a carnival ride she couldn't exit.

Through the vertigo, she fixated on the woman's pendant earrings—delicate silver crescents that glowed with their own soft light. Probably just LED jewelry, the rational part of her brain supplied, though it sounded unconvincing even to herself.

The woman's expression shifted into equal parts apology and reassurance. "It's going to be okay," she said, her voice barely above a whisper. "I just gave you the Gift."

The words floated in the air between them, meaningless yet somehow monumental. Leigh stared at those glowing earrings, her mind desperately fixating on their odd light in the midst of whatever was happening to her reality. She tried to stand, to demand an explanation, but the woman was already moving toward the door. By the time Leigh managed to force her mouth into forming words, the bell had chimed and the mysterious woman was gone.

When she attempted to rise to follow, the floor tilted treacherously, forcing her back into her chair. She gripped the edge of the table, focusing on the solid wood beneath her fingers, willing the world to stop its nauseating dance. Time stretched like taffy—it could have been minutes or hours before the room finally settled into its proper dimensions and her body remembered how to follow basic commands.

Leigh eventually made her way to her car on shaky legs, her mind spinning with questions she couldn't even properly formulate. *What the hell just happened in there?*

THE FIRST WAVE hit her somewhere between Reading and Hartford. The story crashed into her consciousness like a fever dream, except she wasn't hallucinating or having a stroke or suffering some delayed reaction to Matt's dubious pharmaceuticals. No—this was pure creation, a story downloading directly into her brain with crystalline clarity.

Leigh gripped the steering wheel tighter as the scenes unfurled. A train platform in autumn. A woman clutching a gin flask disguised as a poetry book. And there she was: Dahlia Monroe, fully formed, brewing illicit love potions in a converted Victorian mansion while trying to outrun her own disaster of a love life. Leigh could see her so clearly—the way she hid her magic behind vintage dresses and carefully curated normalcy, the slight tremor in her hands when she measured ingredients, her tendency to test her own products after one too many G&Ts.

The story poured out faster than Leigh could process it.

Danfeld Hills materialized in her mind: not just another generic village, but a place with history simmering beneath its quaint surface. She saw the tangled relationships between founding families, the secret passages hidden in colonial-era houses, the way magic threaded through everything like a half-remembered dream. And at the center of it all, The Crimson Kettle—Reg Preston's tavern, with its worn wooden bar and walls that had absorbed a century of whispered secrets.

Red taillights flashed ahead. Leigh hit the brakes and swerved over into the breakdown lane, her heart racing from more than the near miss. She fumbled for her phone, fingers shaking as she opened her notes app. The details were still coming: Dahlia's best friend Bittie Galin, stubbornly ignoring her own magical abilities while running the town's only bookstore (which had a habit of rearranging its shelves according to readers' unspoken needs). A black cat named Malkin who spoke exclusively in literary quotations. The Circean Priestesses who maintained order through a complex system of favors and obligations.

The murder victim appeared next—not some generic corpse, but Matriarch Eleanor Guilfoyle, whose death would force Dahlia to choose between exposing magic to solve the crime or protecting her community's secrets. Leigh could already feel the tension between Dahlia's attraction to Reg (solid, dependable, utterly mortal) and her complicated relationship with Kevyn, the gorgeous badass witch detective with warlock energy whose unexpected presence complicated everything.

This wasn't like her previous attempts at paranormal romance, with their careful market analysis and color-coded plot outlines. This story felt real and chaotic, as though she'd stumbled upon an actual place and was simply taking dictation from its inhabitants. Every character arrived with their own voice, their own desires, their own secrets. They weren't just plot devices or genre requirements—they were people, as real to her now as her own reflection in the rearview mirror.

She typed frantically, trying to capture everything before it could slip away. The themes emerged organically: self-discovery versus self-preservation, the weight of family obligations, the terror and exhilaration of finally embracing one's true nature.

The sun had shifted noticeably by the time Leigh pulled back onto the highway. Her phone was filled with scattered notes and half-finished scenes, but everything felt secure now, anchored in her consciousness. The strange encounter at the coffee shop had already taken on a dreamlike quality. But *The Witch on the Train* remained crystal clear, more vivid than her actual memories of the past twenty-four hours.

She couldn't explain where it had come from. The story defied her usual analytical approach to writing, emerging fully formed like Athena from Zeus's forehead (a reference Malkin would undoubtedly quote at some inappropriate moment). All she knew with absolute certainty was that this was the book she needed to write—not because the market demanded it or because she was trying to please an agent, but because these characters wouldn't leave her alone until she did.

For the first time since opening that last rejection letter, Leigh felt something dangerously close to hope. She merged into the fast lane, Hartford's familiar skyline rising ahead. Whatever had happened in that coffee shop—stroke, hallucination, or something she didn't have words for yet—had cracked open something inside her. The only question was whether she could get it all down on paper before real life tried to stitch her back into her sensible shape.

nine

. . .

The Dragons Had Been Purple

THE SIGHT of her grandmother's writing desk blocking most of her apartment hallway stopped Leigh mid-step. The dark mahogany surface gleamed under the fluorescent lights, making the industrial carpeting look even more depressing by comparison. A yellow Post-it note clung to one corner, Noah's familiar scrawl visible even from a distance:

Moving truck comes tomorrow. -N.

She traced her fingers along the desk's edge, muscle memory finding the faded magic marker stains from the illustrated stories she'd created at twelve. Grandma Margaret had never scolded her about the rainbow of permanent ink bleeding into the mahogany—she'd just asked what happened next in the story. The desk felt larger than Leigh remembered, though maybe her apartment building's hallway had shrunk in the hours she'd been gone. Its presence created a surreal disruption in the utilitarian space, like finding an oil painting hanging in a parking garage.

"It's been there since this morning," Mrs. Chen called from her doorway, her voice carrying the weary resignation of someone who'd spent all day navigating around antique furniture. "The DoorDash man had to leave my lunch on it." She paused, adjusting her cardigan with precise movements. "Your ex-husband's new girlfriend seemed very…efficient."

Efficient. The word burned like acid. Leigh could picture Ellie orchestrating the desk's removal, probably while planning her perfect craft room renovation. The image collided with the story still unfolding in her mind—Dahlia's magical bookshop, the murder mystery, Kevyn's knowing smirk. Reality and fiction blurred at the edges, leaving her unsteady.

"I'm really sorry about the inconvenience," Leigh managed, falling back on the polite professionalism that had become her default setting. "I'll get it inside." The words came out steady, even as her hand remained on the desk's surface, refusing to break contact.

Her fingers found the almost invisible seam of the secret compartment—the one where Grandma Margaret had kept her secret stash that no one else in the family knew about.

Even now, Leigh could perfectly recall the thrill of being the only one trusted with her grandmother's hidden vices— the romance novels her grandfather would have disapproved of (if he was still alive), the cigarettes she'd sneak on the back porch while everyone thought she was tending her roses. God, she'd thought her grandmother was the coolest person alive back then.

"Every woman needs her secrets," Grandma Margaret had told her with a conspiratorial wink, offering twelve-year-old Leigh a cookie while tucking her latest Johanna Lindsey novel deeper into the desk drawer. The words had carried a weight of wisdom Leigh hadn't understood then, though she'd felt impossibly grown-up being trusted with her grandmother's private world. Strange how those afternoons of shared stories and secrets had shaped her more than she'd realized. Now here she was, all those years later, trying to write the kind of romance novel Grandma Margaret would have hidden in that desk.

Mrs. Chen's door clicked shut, leaving Leigh alone with the physical embodiment of her past life blocking her path forward. She could practically hear Dahlia's voice in her head, offering sardonic commentary about symbolic obstacles. The thought startled a laugh from her throat—here she was, having imaginary conversations with her fictional witch while standing in a hallway that smelled like someone's overcooked microwave dinner.

Twenty minutes of effort and creative swearing later, Leigh managed to drag the desk inside. The classic piece made her existing furniture look even more temporary than usual, like props arranged around the only real object in the room. She circled the desk slowly, remembering the week after her grandmother had passed, when the family gathered to divide up Margaret's possessions. Her cousins had claimed the jewelry, the china, the paintings. Leigh had wanted only this desk.

During those first months after inheriting it, she'd spent hours researching its history online, fascinated to discover it was something called a Carlton House desk. The distinctive curved gallery of small drawers along the back had been inspired by a writing table made for the Prince of Wales in the late 1700s. The design was intended for important diplomatic correspondence, though in Margaret's case, it had organized grocery lists, unpaid bills, and her secret novel collection. Brass handles adorned each tiny drawer, their patina telling the story of decades of use. The sliding writing panels could pull out to create an expanded workspace, though the right one always stuck slightly.

The desk dominated her small living room in a way her Instagram-inspired decor never had. Her carefully curated throw blankets, draped artistically over a decorative ladder, suddenly seemed absurd—like trying to make a college dorm room look sophisticated with fairy lights and motivational posters. The ladder would have to go to make room for the desk in the only logical spot: the corner near her balcony's sliding door, where the morning light would hit the wood just right.

When Leigh first brought the desk home to their West Hartford house, Noah had offered to strip and refinish it, suggesting they could eliminate all those magic marker stains from Leigh's childhood storytelling sessions. She'd refused immediately, horrified at the thought. Those faded marks were the best part—physical evidence of where her writing life had begun, back when she'd spent hours crafting illustrated stories about magical princesses while Grandma Margaret sat by the window.

Moving the desk into position felt like wrestling with fate itself. The desk seemed to resist its new home, catching on the carpet, refusing to slide those final few inches into place. But when it finally settled into its corner, the fading sunlight streaming through the sliding glass door and warming the wood to a deep honey color, something inside Leigh settled too. The desk's presence felt right in a way she couldn't explain—like finding the correct word in a sentence after trying dozens of almost-right ones.

Leigh lowered herself into her Target office chair, its fake leather squeaking in protest. The sound felt almost offensive next to the desk's quiet dignity. She made a mental note to check Facebook Marketplace for something more appropriate —preferably something that wouldn't make her grandmother's ghost wince every time she sat down.

Her fingers traced one particularly vivid magic marker stain near the right corner: the remnants of an illustrated story about a family of dragons (the dragons had been purple, if she remembered correctly, though the marker had faded to a murky brown). The contact sent a jolt through her palm, not entirely unlike that strange moment at the coffee shop. But this sensation felt different—less like reality bending and more like pieces clicking into place.

She opened her laptop, its startup chime mixing with the familiar sounds of her neighbor's evening routine (something with a heavy bass line that normally drove her crazy). The desk seemed to anchor her against the city's constant noise, creating a bubble of possibility in her too-small apartment.

The Word document's cursor blinked expectantly. For once, Leigh didn't feel the urge to open yet another spreadsheet analyzing witch romance tropes. Instead, her fingers found the keys with surprising certainty:

```
Dahlia Monroe's love potions were
completely illegal and absolutely guaran-
teed to work. The Victorian mansion's
converted kitchen held enough banned
substances to get her excommunicated from
three different covens, but her waiting
list stretched into next year. Rich women
from Boston's Back Bay ordered her brews by
the case, disguising them in Chanel perfume
bottles and crystal decanters. They never
asked questions about the ingredients, and
Dahlia never volunteered that information.
Everyone stayed happy, or at least magi-
cally convinced of their happiness, which
was basically the same thing.
```

The words flowed with unexpected ease. This wasn't the beginning of her story—that would involve a train platform and a flask disguised as a poetry book—but it didn't matter. She could feel the whole narrative taking shape: Dahlia's barely legal potion shop, her chaotic personal life, the way she tested her own products after one too many gin and tonics.

The desk's smooth surface felt warm under her elbows as she leaned forward, deeper into the story. Even her usually cramped shoulders relaxed, as if the furniture itself was adjusting her posture. Grandma Margaret had always claimed the desk had been in the family for generations, passed down through a line of "difficult women who knew their own minds." At age twelve, Leigh had rolled her eyes at this pronouncement. Now, watching words appear on her screen with almost supernatural ease, she wondered if the old wood held more history than she'd suspected.

The next few hours disappeared into a blur of typing and alcohol. When she finally looked up, darkness had settled over Hartford, and her word count had somehow crossed ten thousand. She saved the document three times (old habits died hard) before crawling into bed, her mind still buzzing with scenes and dialogue that refused to quiet down.

ten

. . .

Maybe That's How It's Supposed to Feel

LEIGH'S CURSOR hovered over the word "migraine" in her email to Sharon. Her head did feel strange—not exactly painful, but buzzing with scenes and dialogue that demanded to be written down. The dim glow of her laptop at 5:30 a.m. cast shadows across her living room, where discarded Salem tourist brochures still littered the coffee table.

Calling in sick to write about a witch with a drinking problem. *Super professional.*

She hit send before her conscience could kick in, then started in on a new chapter:

```
Love potions smell different to everyone.
Fresh bread, newly mown grass, your grand-
mother's perfume—whatever brings you
comfort. But they all share one note under-
neath: desperation. That's how you know
they're working.
```

Dahlia's voice emerged fully formed, nothing like the forced attempts of her previous drafts. The character felt real:

a witch who could brew perfect love potions for others but couldn't manage her own love life, drowning her magical talents in gin while her talking cat watched with judgment. The words poured out faster than Leigh could type them.

The mysterious death of Mrs. Guilfoyle (suspicious herb garden, even more suspicious book collection) spilled onto the page. Reg's tavern materialized with impossible detail—the worn brass rail along the bar, the way the floorboards creaked in specific spots, the dartboard that never hung quite straight no matter how many times he adjusted it.

Her phone buzzed sometime around noon. Dawn's text asked if she needed anything—her work friend's maternal instincts probably triggered by Leigh's uncharacteristic sick day. Leigh sent back a quick "feeling better, working from home" without taking her eyes off the screen. She had never lied to Dawn before (well, except about exactly how many glasses of wine she had at last year's holiday party), but this felt different. Necessary.

The light outside her window shifted from morning to afternoon to evening without Leigh really noticing. Her coffee stayed mysteriously hot—she'd meant to get up and microwave it several times but kept getting caught up in scenes. When her stomach finally demanded attention, she ordered pizza online.

The knock startled her. No, the third knock startled her—she'd apparently ignored the first two. The delivery guy (name tag: Marcus) gave her a weird look that suggested her appearance might be as disheveled as it felt.

Back at her laptop, Leigh reached for her notebook—the one where she had been obsessively tracking witch romance tropes last week. She flipped through until she found the page she needed, her excessive organizational system finally paying off. The pizza grew cold beside her as she typed, barely noticing the sun slipping below the horizon.

Her Spotify shuffled to an obscure '90s ballad called "Night Yoga"—the unfamiliar melody nonetheless matching her mood perfectly. Leigh had been hunting for the right writing music all day, and somehow the algorithm had nailed it. Her fingers paused on the keyboard. The playlist was doing that thing again, serving up exactly what she needed without her having to search. Maybe she should check her settings—had she accidentally enabled some new "read your mind" feature?

The words flowed more easily than they had in months. She found herself instinctively scrolling to earlier passages when she needed to check details, muscle memory from endless rereading kicking in. Even her usual struggles with timeline consistency seemed manageable tonight. Everything just worked, like her brain had finally sorted out all the pieces while she wasn't looking.

You're just in the zone, she told herself. *Flow state. Runner's high for writers*. Leigh had read about this in that productivity book Dawn kept recommending—something about optimal performance conditions aligning. The rational explanation felt a bit forced, but it beat the alternative of questioning her own sanity.

But as midnight approached and her word count crossed 30,000, she couldn't shake the feeling that something fundamental had shifted. The story wasn't coming from her careful planning or analytical research. It felt more like transcribing something that already existed, like taking dictation from a particularly chatty ghost.

Ghost. *Great word choice, Leigh. Really helping with the whole 'everything is normal' theory.*

She forced herself to save the document (three times, because apparently the brush with creativity hadn't cured her OCD) and close her laptop. Tomorrow she'd have to face Sharon and a backlog of actual work. But for now, she sat in her quiet apartment, watching shadows play across the walls and wondering if they'd always moved quite that way.

LIGHT CREPT into the apartment as Tuesday morning arrived, catching Leigh still hunched over her laptop. Nearly 70,000 words of *The Witch on the Train* glowed on her screen, including a fully realized Bittie Galin, who kept insisting her uncanny ability to locate lost objects was "just paying attention, bitch—unlike some people." The character felt so real that Leigh could practically smell her lavender hand cream and hear her excessive attitude—a thought that made her wonder if she'd finally cracked from sleep deprivation.

Her Good Employee brain attempted a weak protest as she composed another 'out sick' email to Sharon. Food poisoning this time—technically possible from that delivery pizza. The excuse felt hollow, like everything about her job lately. In four years at Roxawan, Leigh had never missed two consecutive days without a doctor's note. But her fingers typed out the message anyway—the story's gravitational pull stronger than any corporate obligation.

The intensity of her focus worried her. She'd been writing for—how many hours now? The empty coffee cups scattered across her desk suggested at least six, though her neck hadn't started cramping yet. Strange. Her upstairs neighbor's usual bass-heavy music filtered through the ceiling, accompanied by the rhythmic thud of footsteps that normally drove her crazy. Today, she barely registered them.

Maybe I'm having some kind of breakdown, she thought, staring at her reflection in the laptop screen. That would explain both the maniacal writing pace and her sudden ability to tune out all the usual distractions. She'd produced 280 pages about a witch with a gin problem in less time than it usually took her to outline a marketing strategy. Her analytical mind tried to make sense of this burst of creativity, but for once, spreadsheets and logic felt inadequate.

The sound of a key in her front door lock jolted her out of contemplation. Ami burst in with a canvas bag that smelled promisingly of chicken soup, then stopped short.

"Jesus Christ, Leigh."

Leigh followed her friend's gaze around the apartment, seeing it suddenly through outside eyes. Empty coffee cups colonized every surface like ceramic mushrooms. Takeout containers formed a modern art installation on her coffee table. Overflowing ashtrays dotted every flat surface—she'd abandoned her usual balcony spot days ago, unwilling to be separated from the laptop for even the length of a cigarette. The smell of stale smoke hung in the air, mixing with coffee and desperation in a way that reminded her uncomfortably of her senior year at college. Post-it notes covered the walls in a rainbow explosion of plot points and character details. The index cards tracking Danfeld Hills' magical rules looked suspiciously like her old marketing campaign flowcharts, right down to the color coding system she'd borrowed from her Medicare Advantage presentations.

Leigh became suddenly aware that she was still wearing Sunday's clothes, and her hair felt like it had developed its own ecosystem. *God, I've become one of those crazy writers who forget to shower*, she thought. *At least I'm finally acting the part.*

"Have you slept?" Ami asked, surveying the chaos with the same expression she used when evaluating her students' finger painting experiments.

"I'm fine," Leigh said, but her voice came out in a croak. "I just need to finish this chapter where Dahlia explains the magical properties of gin." Even to her own ears, this didn't sound as reasonable as she'd intended.

"Okay, that's it." Ami snapped the laptop closed with terrifying decisiveness. "You're taking a break."

While Ami heated soup in the kitchen (performing minor miracles of organization to clear counter space), Leigh tried to explain about her drive home from Salem. About how the whole story had appeared in her mind, fully formed, like remembering something she'd always known but somehow forgotten. The words tumbled out—about Dahlia's gin-soaked attempts at love potions, about the murder that threatens to expose her magic, about the whole vibrant world of Danfeld Hills.

She caught herself before mentioning the strange encounter at Wilma's or the way reality had seemed to blur around the edges. That sounded crazy, even in her current sleep-deprived state, and would have to wait for another day. Instead, she pulled up the document on her laptop, where she'd been typing frantically since getting home.

"I know it sounds weird," Leigh said, watching Ami navigate through the maze of coffee cups and takeout containers to set down two bowls of soup. "But it's like… I'm not making any of it up. I'm just writing down what's already there."

"Maybe that's how it's supposed to feel," Ami said, settling into the chair across from her. "You know, when you stop overthinking everything and just let the story be what it wants to be."

Leigh opened her mouth to respond, but the words caught in her throat. She wrapped her hands around her coffee mug, the ceramic cold against her palms. Her mind felt electric with possibilities, humming with scenes and dialogue she hadn't known existed until this moment. The sensation was almost frightening in its intensity.

Eventually, Ami left with Leigh's reluctant promise to shower and sleep. Both seemed like reasonable suggestions, backed by the physical evidence of coffee stains on her worn Bryant sweatshirt and the gritty feeling behind her eyelids. But the moment the door closed, Leigh reopened her laptop.

Words were already forming, demanding to be captured: Dahlia's romantic "meet cute" with Reg Preston, the warm golden light of his tavern, the spark of recognition between two people trying very hard to seem ordinary. Her fingers flew across the keyboard, chasing the story before it could slip away.

eleven

. . .

A 23% Drop in Engagement

LEIGH'S HEELS clicked against the polished floors of Roxawan Insurance's lobby on Wednesday morning, her laptop bag heavier with the weight of her new manuscript. Her inbox resembled a digital disaster zone, and Sharon's three voicemails about the Instagram campaign carried increasing notes of desperation. But for the first time since taking this job, the sight of her crowded calendar didn't make her want to run for the emergency exit.

Nearly three hundred pages in two days, she thought, running her fingers over her laptop. *Maybe I really am a writer and not just playing one on Instagram.*

The morning marketing meeting started normally enough—fluorescent lights buzzing overhead, Brad from Digital Optimization fumbling with his presentation software. Leigh's attention drifted between her laptop screen and the half-finished chapter she'd been working on at 4 a.m. The lack of sleep left her feeling oddly disconnected, like she was watching everything through a slightly warped lens.

"Our Q1 numbers show—" Brad began.

"A 23% drop in engagement," Leigh offered, the prediction based on the trends she'd been tracking in her own spreadsheets for months. The statistical analysis part of her brain never really turned off, even when she'd rather be thinking about Dahlia's latest magical mishap.

Brad stared at her, then clicked to his next slide. There it was: 23% exactly. Leigh's coffee cup wobbled as her hand trembled slightly—a combination of too much caffeine and too little sleep. She steadied it quickly, avoiding what could have been a professionally devastating coffee tsunami across her quarterly reports.

That's what happens when you stay up writing until dawn, her rational brain chided. *You start seeing patterns everywhere, like some marketing savant gone rogue.*

Her quiet self-recrimination was interrupted by Sharon appearing at her desk after the meeting, radiating the kind of forced casualness that made Leigh's stomach clench. The promotion offer still hung between them, unanswered.

"About our discussion last week..." Sharon began, perching on the edge of Leigh's desk like they were about to have a fun girl chat instead of a serious career path conversation.

Leigh was about to launch into her carefully prepared food poisoning story as an excuse about why she hadn't yet responded, but the words died in her throat. Knowledge hit her like a physical blow: *Sharon was pregnant. Two months along. Morning sickness masquerading as stress. Hadn't told anyone yet, not even her husband.* The information felt as solid and real as the desk under her hands.

"Actually," Sharon said, lowering her voice to almost a whisper, "I wanted to tell you something first. I'm... pregnant."

Leigh gripped the arms of her chair, her knuckles white. "Two months?" she heard herself ask.

Sharon's eyes widened. "How did you...?" She shook her

head. "Never mind. Yes. I haven't told anyone else yet. The morning sickness has been…challenging. Let's continue this in my office."

Following Sharon into her office felt like walking into a trap of Leigh's own making. The familiar space—with its artfully arranged family photos and ruthlessly organized desk—had hosted countless strategy sessions. But today the walls seemed to press closer, heavy with expectations and secrets.

Sharon shut the door and settled into her chair, one hand drifting unconsciously to her stomach. A week ago, Leigh would have missed that gesture entirely. Now it felt charged with meaning.

"Congratulations," Leigh said, the word escaping before she could stop it. "I mean, about the baby."

"Thank you." Sharon's smile carried equal parts joy and anxiety. "It was…unexpected. The doctors keep using terms like 'geriatric pregnancy' because I'm thirty-seven, if you can believe that."

Leigh's mind wandered to their company health insurance coverage (geriatric at thirty-seven, really?) before snapping back to the present as Sharon continued.

"I didn't want to mention it the other day, but this actually makes our conversation about the Senior Marketing Manager role more urgent," Sharon said. "We have aggressive targets for next year, and I need the new department structure running perfectly before…" She trailed off, but Leigh's treacherous intuition filled in the gaps: *before morning sickness gets worse, before maternity leave, before everything changes.*

The peppermint tea on Sharon's desk (replacing her usual double espresso) filled the air with its sharp, clean scent. Leigh cataloged it as yet another sign she should have noticed earlier.

"I have to know your decision, Leigh." Sharon leaned

forward, her expression earnest. "You're exactly who I need in this role. Someone who understands both the creative and analytical sides of what we do."

The wrongness of saying yes hit Leigh like a physical wave. Her manuscript seemed to burn in her laptop bag, demanding attention. The story that had poured out of her for the past forty-eight hours felt more real than all the quarterly projections and ROI analyses scattered across Sharon's desk.

"I want to help," Leigh heard herself saying, "but I have some personal matters going on right now. Family stuff." The lie tasted bitter, but it was easier than explaining about witches and talking cats and impossible knowledge flooding her brain. "I want to be completely certain I can honor any commitments I make."

Sharon nodded in what Leigh hoped was grudging respect. "That kind of conscientiousness is exactly why you're right for this position," Sharon said. "How much time do you need to sort things out?"

"Friday," Leigh promised, desperate to escape the suffocating weight of expectations. "I'll have an answer by Friday."

In the relative safety of the third-floor bathroom, Leigh braced herself against the sink. Her reflection stared back, pale but unchanged. Shouldn't there be some visible sign of whatever was happening to her? The fluorescent lights buzzed overhead as fragments of that strange encounter at Wilma's coffee shop replayed in her mind.

I just gave you the Gift.

The words echoed differently now, carrying the weight of prophecy instead of confusion. Leigh's careful categories of possible and impossible were dissolving, leaving her with nothing but questions and a growing certainty that accepting the promotion would be like closing a door she might never find again.

She splashed cold water on her face, but it did nothing to

wash away the feeling that her orderly life had spun irretrievably off its axis. The worst part wasn't the strange new abilities or even the desperate creative drive—it was the growing suspicion that this chaos might actually be leading her exactly where she needed to go.

twelve

. . .

A Prediction and a Promise

THE NUMBERS GLOWED on Leigh's screen at 1:49 a.m.: 86,753 words. *Done.*

Her fingers still trembled slightly from too much coffee and this final push. Over seven straight hours of writing in a fever dream, switching from wine to gin because somehow it helped her channel Dahlia's voice better. (*Not at all because you're starting to think like a fictional witch,* she told herself firmly).

The novel's climactic scene still blazed in her mind: Dahlia confronting old Mrs. Guilfoyle's ghost in the tavern cellar, the failed immortality potion giving off toxic green smoke, dark and sexy Kevyn arriving just in time with the correct magical antidote. But it was the quiet scene afterward that kept replaying—Dahlia and Kevyn in the kitchen, the air between them charged with more than just residual magic.

Leigh had written several romantic scenes before, but this one felt different. Even though she had never experienced it personally, she somehow understood with perfect clarity that rush of recognition when you found someone who didn't just see you, but understood the specific way you moved through the world. It was like another kind of magic entirely

—not the showy kind, but something deeper and more fundamental.

She found herself moved by the profound intimacy of two women who'd been taught all their lives to make themselves smaller, finally allowing themselves to take up space together.

Where did that insight come from? she wondered. Certainly not from binge-watching every episode of *The L Word* with Ami.

The entire manuscript hummed with that same sense of authenticity and truth, as if the story had existed long before she started typing, just waiting for her to get out of its way. Her previous novels had been careful constructions. This one seemed to have arrived fully formed, like a gift. (*The Gift*, her mind whispered, but she pushed that thought away. One impossible thing at a time).

Leigh stared at her phone, thumb hovering over Ami's contact. The story wasn't really finished until Ami read it. Her friend's opinion mattered more than any agent's.

The text composed itself:

> It's done. 86k words of love & witchiness. You are my first reader! But please hurry— need to get it to the agent ASAP

She hit send.

Her phone buzzed almost immediately. Ami's name lit up the screen, accompanied by the ridiculous contact photo from their fake anniversary dinner at Salute last year. Guilt stabbed through Leigh's post-writing euphoria. "God, I didn't mean to wake you—"

"Bold of you to assume I sleep like a normal person," Ami cut in, her voice carrying that particular mix of exhaustion and forced cheer that Leigh recognized all too well. "I'm just watching cooking shows and wondering why I can't make a soufflé rise. Send me your witch book."

"You have to be at school in—" Leigh checked her laptop

clock, wincing, "five hours. Take one of those gummies you swear by and get some actual rest. The book isn't going anywhere."

"I'm already up, and now I'm invested. Besides, the kids have art history tomorrow—they can watch a video about Erin Hanson while I read about sexy witches."

Something in Ami's voice made Leigh pause, her inner analyst noting the slight tremor that suggested this wasn't just regular insomnia. But before she could ask, Ami added, "Stop overthinking and send the damn book, Leigh."

"Fine, but don't blame me when you're falling asleep during class tomorrow."

She pulled up her email, attaching the manuscript with trembling fingers. Her cursor hovered over the send button as a wave of vulnerability crashed over her. This wasn't just sharing her writing anymore—it was like handing Ami the key to rooms in her mind she hadn't even known existed until three days ago.

"You still there?" Ami asked softly.

"Yeah, just…" Leigh took a deep breath. "It's different from my usual stuff. Maybe too different."

"Good. Your usual stuff was trying too hard to be what other people wanted. Send it."

Leigh clicked send before she could change her mind. The whoosh of the email departing felt momentous, like she'd just cast a spell of her own. "It's done. No taking it back now."

"Perfect. Now go to sleep, you crazy witch."

"That's rich coming from you, insomniac artist."

Their familiar banter felt reassuringly normal, even as Leigh's new manuscript sat in Ami's inbox like a confession she hadn't meant to make.

THE NEXT MORNING, Leigh stretched lazily in bed, savoring the strange sensation of being actually rested instead of just gin-numb and coffee-wired. She couldn't remember the last time she'd fallen asleep before midnight, let alone stayed asleep until morning.

Her apartment buzzer's angry sound shattered the peaceful moment.

"Hey, let me up!" Ami's voice crackled through the ancient intercom. "I have coffee and those almond croissants you pretend not to like."

Leigh buzzed her in, then stared at the clock with growing concern. Seven a.m. on a weekday meant Ami should have been at school, playing that art video for her kids. The last time she'd skipped school was when her pet ferret died. Leigh's stomach clenched as she pulled on her robe, mentally cataloging everything that could have gone wrong.

Ami burst through the door in a whirlwind of coffee cups and paper bags. Behind her glasses, her eyes had the manic gleam that was a little scary. "I finished it," she announced, shoving a coffee into Leigh's hands. "Pulled an all-nighter. Thanks for that, by the way. I have nineteen text messages from my students' parents about why art class is canceled today."

"Canceled? You didn't have to—"

"Are you kidding? I couldn't put it down. Like, not even to pee." Ami paced the living room, coffee sloshing danger-ously close to the rim of her mug. "It's soooooo good. The whole Greniere family dynamic? The way Thad and Hicks basically adopt Dahlia even though she's fighting it the whole time? God, and the murder mystery—I kept thinking I knew who did it, but then you'd throw in another twist. I stayed up until four because I had to know if Reg was actually involved. Then I had to power through to the end."

"It's just a first draft—"

"Stop. Just stop." Ami planted herself directly in front of

Leigh, her expression fierce. "The way you write Dahlia? She's such a hot mess but I want to be her best friend. I love her. I really do. And that scene where she finally admits to Kevyn that her love potions never work on the people she actually wants them to? I full-on sobbed."

"Thank you—" Leigh started, but Ami waved the words away with her coffee cup.

"Also," Ami said, sinking onto the couch and tucking her feet under her like she always did when settling in for a serious conversation. "For someone who's only dated guys, you kind of really nailed the girl stuff." She studied Leigh's face with exaggerated intensity. "Are you holding out on me?"

"Shut up." Leigh felt her cheeks warming.

"Just saying…" Ami's lips curved into a teasing smile. "It seemed pretty authentic…"

Leigh laughed. "I just wrote them as two people who fall in love. The rest…" She shrugged, remembering how naturally their story had flowed onto the page. "It wasn't even something I thought about. They just were who they were."

"Well, whatever your secret is, it works." Ami leaned forward, eyes bright with caffeine and enthusiasm. "That scene when Kevyn helps Dahlia with her necklace in the herb shop? I had to put the book down and walk around my apartment. And don't even get me started on that truth serum thing. By the time they finally get together, I was practically screaming into my pillow."

Leigh sank onto the couch beside Ami, warmth spreading through her chest that had nothing to do with the coffee. "Thank you. Really." The words felt inadequate for what Ami had given her—not just reading the entire manuscript in one night, but understanding exactly what she'd been trying to create. "Though I still feel terrible about your students missing art class."

"Those kids needed a mental health day anyway. Do you

know how many tissue paper flowers I've had to untangle from the blinds this week?" Ami took a big drink of coffee, even though she obviously didn't need the caffeine. "So what's the next step? Because if you tell me you're planning to sit on this for six months while you overthink every sentence, I swear I'll email it myself."

The familiar flutter of submission anxiety tickled Leigh's stomach, but for once it felt more like anticipation than dread. "Actually…" She took a fortifying sip of coffee. "I'm sending it to Dawn's sister today. Going to beg her to at least read the first five pages before Friday."

"What's happening Friday?"

"Judgment Day." At Ami's confused look, Leigh sighed. "Sharon needs my final answer about the promotion. The Senior Marketing Manager position. I have to commit one way or another."

"The agent's going to love it." Ami's confidence felt like a warm blanket. "This time next year, your book will be in Barnes & Noble displays across the country. *The Witch on the Train* by Leigh Dolan, right there on the cover in big type."

"Actually…" Leigh picked at a loose thread on her sleeve, a habit she thought she'd broken years ago. "I'm using a pen name. Morgan L.F. Mallory."

Ami's eyebrows shot up. "Ooh, very witchy. Where'd that come from?"

The name had appeared in Leigh's mind fully formed, like everything else about this book. "Same place all of it came from," she said quietly. The memory of pink-streaked hair and glowing earrings flickered through her mind.

Ami launched herself across the couch, wrapping Leigh in a fierce hug. "Well, Morgan Mallory," she said, her voice muffled against Leigh's shoulder, "this book is going to be huge. Like, seriously huge."

The certainty in Ami's voice matched the feeling that had been growing in Leigh's chest since typing that final sentence.

It wasn't her usual careful market analysis or her spreadsheet-backed optimism. This felt different—like knowledge rather than hope, as real as the warmth of Ami's arms around her or the lingering scent of gin in her empty glass.

"I think you're right," Leigh whispered, allowing herself to lean into the hug for just a moment longer than usual. "I think it's going to change everything. For both of us."

The words felt like both a prediction and a promise, carrying the same weight as that strange encounter at Wilma's coffee shop.

Leigh wondered if this was what it felt like to cast a spell —speaking truth into existence, letting go of the careful plans and safety nets she'd built her life around.

For once, the thought didn't terrify her.

author's note

If you've made it this far, first of all—thank you. You've just closed the book on one mystery, but I can promise you, Gina Biletti's story is far from over. In fact there are three more novels in the series, already written and in the queue for publication.

In Book Six, *Murder at the Med-Spa*, Gina trades the cozy streets of Maidenwell for the bright lights (and sharper shadows) of Los Angeles. What starts as a "treat yourself" trip to a luxury med-spa—new city, new glow, new Gina—takes a nightmarish turn when when a minor celeb is found murdered in one of the treatment rooms.

Imagine: chilled cucumber water, designer robes, and the faint scent of lavender diffusers…interrupted by flashing police lights and Detective Ferris Saito's suspicious side-eye. Gina is groggy from her own procedure, suddenly caught between Botox parties and back-alley blackmail, wondering if beauty really is worth dying for.

Expect celebrity soirées, questionable serums, and a mystery wrapped in LA glamour—with Gina at the center, balancing reinvention, temptation, and danger. There's a new journalist ally, an old friend by her side, and maybe (just maybe) a screenwriter who's a little too charming for his own good.

I can't wait for you to follow Gina into this next chapter—where the real question isn't just *whodunit,* but *who do you become when the mask comes off?*

See you in LA. Bring sunscreen.

—BGW

P.S. Some mysteries won't wait for the next book—and my email subscribers are the very first to hear about them. That means free short stories and novellas you can't get anywhere else (including *The Opportunity* and the upcoming *The Last Train to Maidenwell*), plus behind-the-scenes extras like character portraits, recipes, story podcasts, and other background pieces that connect the dots between Gina's adventures.

If you'd like to be in on Gina's next mystery the moment it's revealed—subscribe for free at:

murderwell.com/subscribe

Library of Congress Cataloging-in-Publication Data
Name: Wood, B.G., author
Title: Witchnapped: a novella / B.G. Wood
Description: First edition | Oregon: Bogwood Press, 2025
Subjects: GSAFD: Detective and mystery fiction

Name: Wood, B.G., author
Title: The Gift: a novella / B.G. Wood
Description: First edition | Oregon: Bogwood Press, 2025
Subjects: GSAFD: Detective and mystery fiction

murderwell.com